P9-CCP-676

Acclaim for
Your House Is on Fire, Your Children All Gone

"Full of dark folk magic and frightful, lurid wonder. It casts a spell, winking all the way through every grim detail and shadowy secret." —Paul Elwork, author of
The Girl Who Would Speak for the Dead

"Creepy in a way that actually made me quite nervous."
—Ben Loory, author of
Stories for Nighttime and Some for the Day

"A brilliant amalgam of Faulkner, the Brothers Grimm, and Günter Grass as if condensed for intensity."
—Josip Novakovich, author of
Fiction Writer's Workshop and *Writing Fiction Step by Step*

"The characters are all doomed. 'Doomed to what?' is the only question, and you won't put the book down until you find out."
—Christopher Buehlman, author of
Those Across the River and *Between Two Fires*

"[A novel] with a chilling twist here and there, a sly, stark wit, and a fascinating cast of lost boys and girls."
—Timothy Schaffert, author of *The Coffins of Little Hope*

"Stefan Kiesbye would be a writer to watch out for if he had not so clearly already arrived."
—Daniel Woodrell, author of *Winter's Bone*

ABOUT THE AUTHOR

STEFAN KIESBYE has an MFA in creative writing from the University of Michigan. Born on the German coast of the Baltic Sea, he moved to Berlin in the early 1980s. He studied drama and worked in radio before starting a degree in American studies, English, and comparative literature at Berlin's Freie Universität. A scholarship brought him to Buffalo, New York, in 1996. Kiesbye now lives in Portales, New Mexico, where he teaches creative writing at Eastern New Mexico University. He is also the arts editor of *Absinthe: New European Writing*. His stories and poems have appeared in numerous magazines and anthologies, and his first book, *Next Door Lived a Girl*, won the Low Fidelity Press Novella Award and was praised by Peter Ho Davies as "utterly gripping," by Charles Baxter as "both laconic and feverish," and by Robert Olmstead as "maddeningly powerful."

Your House Is on Fire, Your Children All Gone

a novel

Stefan Kiesbye

PENGUIN BOOKS

PENGUIN BOOKS
Published by the Penguin Group
Penguin Group (USA) Inc., 375 Hudson Street, New York, New York 10014, U.S.A.
Penguin Group (Canada), 90 Eglinton Avenue East, Suite 700, Toronto, Ontario, Canada
M4P 2Y3 (a division of Pearson Penguin Canada Inc.) · Penguin Books Ltd, 80 Strand,
London WC2R 0RL, England · Penguin Ireland, 25 St Stephen's Green, Dublin 2, Ireland
(a division of Penguin Books Ltd) · Penguin Group (Australia), 250 Camberwell Road,
Camberwell, Victoria 3124, Australia (a division of Pearson Australia Group Pty Ltd) ·
Penguin Books India Pvt Ltd, 11 Community Centre, Panchsheel Park, New Delhi - 110 017,
India · Penguin Group (NZ), 67 Apollo Drive, Rosedale, Auckland 0632, New Zealand
(a division of Pearson New Zealand Ltd) · Penguin Books (South Africa) (Pty) Ltd, 24 Sturdee
Avenue, Rosebank, Johannesburg 2196, South Africa

Penguin Books Ltd, Registered Offices:
80 Strand, London WC2R 0RL, England

Copyright © Stefan Kiesbye, 2012
All rights reserved

Pages 21–30 appeared in different form under the title
"Rico's Journey Through Hell" in *Hobart* in 2007.

Pages 93–103 appeared in different form under the title
"The Mill" in *Fickle Muses* in 2007.

Publisher's Note
This is a work of fiction. Names, characters, places, and incidents either are the product of
the author's imagination or are used fictitiously, and any resemblance to actual persons,
living or dead, business establishments, events, or locales is entirely coincidental.

ISBN 978-0-14-312146-6

Printed in the United States of America
Set in Adobe Garamond
Designed by Elke Sigal

Except in the United States of America, this book is sold subject to the condition that it shall
not, by way of trade or otherwise, be lent, resold, hired out, or otherwise circulated without
the publisher's prior consent in any form of binding or cover other than that in which it is
published and without a similar condition including this condition being imposed on the
subsequent purchaser.

The scanning, uploading and distribution of this book via the Internet or via any other means
without the permission of the publisher is illegal and punishable by law. Please purchase only
authorized electronic editions, and do not participate in or encourage electronic piracy of
copyrighted materials. Your support of the author's rights is appreciated.

ALWAYS LEARNING   PEARSON

For Sanaz Kiesbye, Nils Fahrenholz,
and Don Mitchell

We're a lukewarm people for all our feast days and hard work. Not much touches us, but we long to be touched. We lie awake at night willing the darkness to part and show us a vision. Our children frighten us in their intimacy, but we make sure they grow up like us. Lukewarm like us. On a night like this, hands and faces hot, we can believe that tomorrow will show us angels in jars and that the well-known woods will suddenly reveal another path.

—JEANETTE WINTERSON,
The Passion

It is my belief, Watson, founded upon my experience, that the lowest and vilest alleys in London do not present a more dreadful record of sin than does the smiling and beautiful countryside. . . . Look at these lonely houses, each in its own fields, filled for the most part with poor ignorant folk who know little of the law. Think of the deeds of hellish cruelty, the hidden wickedness which may go on, year in, year out, in such places, and none the wiser.

—SIR ARTHUR CONAN DOYLE,
"The Adventure of the Copper Beeches"

Your House Is on Fire,
Your Children All Gone

Prologue

Time is of no importance. I have returned to Hemmersmoor to live in the same house in which I grew up, the same cramped house in which my father and my sister Ingrid died when I was a schoolboy. I pour water from silver ewers onto their graves and pull weeds and put sweet williams into the soil. From time to time, one of the old villagers asks about them and remembers the incidents from forty years ago. Then their noses start to twitch, as if they smell a fire. Their lips tremble, but the words won't come and they drop the topic immediately. Nobody has ever bothered me about their deaths. I never had anything to hide.

Our village has grown—rich people from Bremen have built vacation homes here, and their immaculately polished cars park every morning in front of Meier's bakery. The noise seems foreign, life seems to have quickened. When I was a boy in Hemmersmoor, our village consisted of the main street and a few alleys and dirt roads. The houses were old and stooped—the doors and windows narrow and low, the beams twisted by rheumatism. The cobblestone was full of humps and holes, and nobody drove through our village just for pleasure. Even the sunlight seemed different, darker, never without suspicion.

When I learned of my mother's death, I lived in Buffalo, New York. I had retired from my work the year before and hadn't heard from my family in decades, had pushed them to the outer limits of my memory and caged them there like wild animals.

The solicitor's letter from Groß Ostensen did not reach me in time to come to the funeral. I've learned that not even my sister Nicole made the trip, and she has not visited the village since. Why I returned, I cannot say or even think. It might have been my wife's death. It was she who gave me a home in the New World. She was my continent, and without her, I was uprooted a second time. Perhaps it was the prospect of stepping into my father's house as its owner. Perhaps I thought the wild animals had died with my mother and I was safe from them now. I had planned to return to the States after two weeks.

Alex Frick, a friend of mine from the past, also lives in Hemmersmoor once again. The sins of his early years are forgiven—or perhaps only forgotten. He is running his father's tavern and is an important man. We are now the old people here, nobody but us remembers his years in the correctional facility, or his brother, Olaf, who almost cost him his inheritance and who one day disappeared forever.

When we meet in the streets, Alex nods. We don't talk much about the past, there's no reason for it. Our secrets in Hemmersmoor were always open and always kept safe. These days the two of us safeguard the stories of our village; we are their caretakers and can change them at any given time. Alex remembers me, Christian, the pale boy whose eyebrows were so light that his face seemed completely naked. He remembers my father, who drank himself to death and whose daughter gave birth to a bastard child. Alex knows that much remains unsaid, but he has better things to do than to rummage through old stories. He expects me to return his favor.

The young people in the village work in factories in Bremen or in stores and factories in Groß Ostensen. The farmers have given up, and the boats that once sailed our canals are now tourist attractions. Hemmersmoor looks colorful and immaculate, as if we were put here for the sake of the hobby photographers. Potters and painters are offering their wares.

The pharmacy, which even decades ago was always freshly painted, still overlooks the village square. The old schoolhouse is still standing, but two families are living there these days. The once sandy school lot is now a multipurpose garden, and a young woman grows vegetables there. Her children's voices tear the silence to shreds.

Just outside the village, near the Droste River, stood Brümmer's tool factory. It was a low-slung building that had served as an ammunitions factory during the last war. In front of Brümmer's, the only railroad track ever to reach Hemmersmoor ended, and in the afternoons the other boys and I sat by the buffer that prevented the cars from rolling into the river and waited for a train to appear.

There was no set timetable, and most days we waited in vain. But still, the mere prospect of catching a glimpse of the small, black steam engine and two or three cars kept us enthralled.

The factory now stands empty; the tracks are covered by tall weeds. A few years back, a fire destroyed what was left of Otto Nubis's workshop. What lay beyond the factory, outside our village, we all have dutifully forgotten. The county is trying to open a museum there, but who is going to buy our paintings and clay souvenirs if their plan is successful? The villagers are shaking their heads. Why should we have to suffer again? We had nothing to do with it.

Time is of no importance. I was young and didn't know a thing about our time. There had never been a different one in Hemmersmoor. In our village time didn't progress courageously. In our village she limped a bit, got lost more than once, and always ended up at Frick's bar and in one of Jens Jensen's tall tales.

Yet now time has made a daring leap. No matter how much I look for them, the dark corners of Hemmersmoor are freshly scrubbed, the wrinkles have been smoothed over, and my memories lead me astray. I have returned, but not to the village I once left. That village doesn't exist anymore, survives in only my memories and dreams. When I walk through our streets at night, blue flickering light can be seen behind every window. I haven't lived under a rock these past decades, but when I think back to my boyhood, there's no room for television.

Now that our village belongs to the ordinary world around it, the pale boy from the past looks like a ghost. Maybe it's for the better, maybe this is what allows me to stay. Maybe I would choke otherwise. But the absence of what I can still see so clearly in front of me makes it hard for me to breathe anyway.

The Big House stands upon the sandy hill that marks the grave of Hüklüt the Giant. He carried a large sack of fine sand, to avoid sinking into the treacherous moor. Yet it didn't matter, and the manor of the von Kamphoff family is his headstone. The gables and turrets, the yellow stone and the gravel driveway—they remain incomprehensible to the villagers.

It's the first time I'm driving out to the Big House. The

spring day is a puppy, unconcerned and playful, and I roll down a window, and the air is soft and ticklish, and I rub my face again and again. Clouds hang low above the moor. It may rain later on but they're still shimmering faintly pink. The grass along the road is already green again.

When my family still lived in Hemmersmoor and Johann von Kamphoff still reigned over the manor, only very few villagers had the pleasure of walking through the gardens or entering the house. From time to time, the von Kamphoffs' black sedan arrived in our village, which seemed much too small for such a car, and most of the time it was Rutger, the old master's grandson, who stepped out of the car and onto our cobblestones to go after one girl or another.

The gardens of the manor are neglected, but the vastness of the property proves the old legend right. The bushes are covered with bright-green spots, and the lawns don't seem to end. In the distance I can make out the maze. Guests at Frick's Inn often whisper that people have disappeared inside; its hedges are thick and impenetrable and higher than the tallest man.

Alex Frick's Opel stands in the gravel courtyard, and he leans against its fender and smokes a cigarette. He's a tall man, a bit stooped by now, bulky but not cloddish. His dark suit is custom tailored; his tie is made from silk. Alex is taking care of his brother's widow, has been married to her for many years, and together they have expanded Frick's Inn. In the summer you can see vacationers on the new terrace, where they sit over strawberry cake and coffee and talk about the picturesque backwater. Alex's eyebrows have grown together, and are almost white, but his face remains boyish. A smile is playing in the corners of his fleshy lips.

"Are you trying to push up the price and jeopardize my business?" he asks and laughs. "You know you can't outbid me. Don't make life harder for me than it already is."

I shake my head. "Are we the only ones?"

He nods toward the road leading down to our village. A small van becomes visible in the distance and slowly makes its way toward us. I know the van. It belongs to our schoolfellow Martin Schürholz. His father, Klaus, once our country constable, is long since dead, and Martin runs a small store in the village, where he sells souvenirs and paintings by local artists.

The manor must have been impressive once, but the courtyard is full of weeds, and weeds and moss are climbing the walls. The yellow stone has blackened and crumbled in places. Some of the windows are missing, and the holes have been filled with cardboard and trash bags. The stables, which stand to our left, have collapsed. "She must have had money enough," I say and shake my head.

Alex gives a short laugh. It sounds like a bark. "Always paid her bill. God knows where she kept that money hidden. In twenty years she never once left the house." I have heard the rumor too, the one about the money still being hidden somewhere, but also the whispered suspicion that Alex is trying to buy the manor only because of the secret treasure.

Martin parks his rusty van and gets out, nodding at us. His hair is red, parted neatly, and he's wearing round wire-rimmed glasses. He joins us reluctantly and accepts the cigarette Alex offers only after a moment of hesitation. Martin is our age, but his trim body makes him look like a schoolboy next to Alex. Sometimes I see him running through the village in yellow trainers. He and his wife never visit Frick's Inn, and they avoid

Alex, even though they are invited to every event at his house. Whenever seeing Alex is unavoidable, Martin shows up by himself.

But today we are paying our respects to our old friend Anke, and together we wait for the hearse from Groß Ostensen. After a few empty exchanges about business and the weather, we fall silent and stare at our cigarettes, as though they contained answers to life's mysteries.

Anke was a proud woman, and she was one of us. She went to school with us, and her mother participated every year in Hemmersmoor's cooking contest. Already as a young girl she had wanted to move into the Big House, and no advice, no tragedy, and no friendship could keep her from reaching that goal. Just like me, she escaped our village, and although the manor was only a few kilometers outside of Hemmersmoor, it was always very much its own world.

After a few minutes, during which Alex has walked around the house and stooped here and there to inspect the walls, a distant roar and rattle startles us out of our thoughts. We haven't expected her, but Linde Janeke is driving toward us in her old Volkswagen. Her hair hasn't been brown for a long time, and her features have suffered just like ours and have lost their sharpness. Yet in Linde's case, her wrinkles hide the scars that once disfigured her. Her dark eyes still sparkle. "Can't complain," she says when Alex asks about her well-being, yet it sounds like a complaint. She looks at Martin and sneers. "You too, Professor? Is Anke really worth such fine company?" Then she squints at the house and the blind-and-broken windows. "What a tragedy," she says and almost looks happy.

Martin decides to ignore Linde's remark and watches her with a mixture of suspicion and contempt. Linde is the only one in our village who's still talking about witches and ghosts. She wears loose-fitting dresses and shirts, which she dyes herself. On some days she points into the air and describes the things none of us can see. Howling dogs and wailing mothers with empty eye sockets. She claims the ghosts confide in her; she claims there are still more things between heaven and hell than the vacationers in our village can imagine. Alex and Martin claim she's lost her mind.

The cemetery of the Big House lies hidden behind tall hedges; the hinges of the gate screech as it swings slowly open. Lime trees offer a little shade, and stone benches stand next to the graves. The old owner and his wife lie buried here, as do their only son and his wife, who, it is said, was once famous in the red-light district of Hamburg's port. And Anke's husband, underneath whose name her own has been waiting for years.

Together we walk toward that small cemetery, and Alex starts searching for a particular headstone. He finds it off to the side, as though it doesn't really belong. It's the grave of his sister, Anna, and her small daughter. "Wouldn't make room for them," he says and picks a few dead branches off the soil. "Not even after their deaths did they know where to put them. And that one"—he points toward the house as though Anke were still living inside—"even moved the headstone once she got here. Didn't want to be reminded of her predecessor." He straightens up again and looks around. "Anna was the mistress of the house, and they made me the chauffeur." He laughs and spits on the ground. He has plans to convert the dilapidated farmhouse into a hotel and riding stable. His lawyers and accountants are already inspecting the von Kamphoffs' accounts.

It was Alex who became aware of Anke's death. It was he

who delivered groceries every Friday to her locked door and picked up the empty crate from the week before, plus a sealed envelope with the money she owed him. "Never saw the old hag," he says. "When they finally forced open the door, one of the cops had to barf. The smell inside was that bad. She didn't bother to find a bathroom anymore."

In the old days, no one from our village would have been invited to attend a funeral here, but today the four of us are the only ones to keep the undertaker and his men company. The black Mercedes bumps over the old road that connects the Big House with Groß Ostensen, and the men get out of the hearse and nod to us. Alex helps them carry the white coffin to the open grave. The family crest has been painted in gold on its sides. Even in death Anke observes strict etiquette.

After the men have lowered the coffin into the grave, the undertaker, a man in a black suit and with thinning hair, says a few words. He talks about solidity, character, a strong will, and a belief in community and charity. He's from Groß Ostensen and doesn't know us. His words come from the well-meaning calendars we get every year for free at the gas station. Alex, Linde, and Martin listen with stern faces, but I think Linde's mouth is twitching from time to time—whether from grief or bemusement I can't say. When the undertaker ends his speech, the grave is filled in. In the background the pink edges of the clouds turn dark and the air smells sweet; perhaps it is the coming rain, perhaps the tastefully gaudy wreath the men lay onto the dark soil.

When the undertaker has gone and the black hearse is back on its way to Groß Ostensen, Linde steps closer to the head-stone, inspects the inscription, and rounds the grave, as though to make sure that Anke won't be able to get out. Her dress is as gaudy as the wreath, only its colors are more washed out. Loudly she coughs up some phlegm and spits it out. "You piece of shit," she says. "There you go." She stomps around on the loose soil.

Alex steps toward her, talks to her, tries to lead her away from the grave, but Linde shakes off his arm. "Go fuck yourself, Alex. Don't get all holy on me now. You couldn't stand her." When he still won't leave her, she slaps him in the face. She has to get up on her toes to do it. "Don't touch me again," she says. "You killed her." With legs wide apart, she bends over, hikes up her skirt, shows us that she isn't wearing any underwear, and pisses onto the grave. Alex shakes his head and brushes his suit with his hands as though it suddenly has become dirty. Martin turns away without a word and walks toward his van. Alex raises one hand and shouts, "Stop by the inn tonight," but Martin doesn't react. Surely he doesn't want to have heard.

"Done," Linde finally says, then lets down her skirt and straightens it. Angrily she stares after Martin's van, until a tiny smile scurries over her face. "The coffin should have had a window. A large, round window. Hell, the whole lid should have been made from glass." Once more, she steps toward the grave and looks at what she's done. "I just hope she can see me from hell." The smile spreads on her face. You could almost call her beautiful.

Martin

In September we celebrated Thanksgiving in Hemmersmoor,* and mass was followed by festivities at Frick's. In the afternoon, after beer stuck to every surface, the villagers spilled into the square to take part in the yearly cooking contest.

"For the first one death, for the second starvation, for the third one bread"—that old proverb described the colonization of the Devil's Moor, but our bread remained as hard and gray and sour as our soil.

To enter the cooking contest was costly, because the rules stated that each dish had to feed at least four dozen people. Hemmersmoor had three categories: best stew, best roast, and best *Butterkuchen*, the buttery, sugar-sprinkled sheet cake our baker, Meier, was famous for and that he sold for funerals and weddings alike. Meier always won the contest, uncontested that is, because who would dare go up against him?

The stew contest was, for the imaginary outsider—there were never any real outsiders present during the cooking contest—an unappetizing affair. You need to have lived in the

---

* German Thanksgiving is celebrated in late September or early October.

North to appreciate *Labskaus*, an old sailor dish, or Pears, Beans, and Bacon, another favorite.

The roast contest was maybe our favorite, and the more contestants entered, the better the feast that followed in the village square. Nobody in the village could resist the doctor's wife's pork roast or help stuffing themselves with beef dished out by the mailman's wife. And this year the competition was unusually fierce and promising. Four families had entered the stew contest, five the roast contest, and Meier faced his first rival in fifteen years—my mother, Käthe Schürholz.

Fueled by compliments on her *Butterkuchen*—my father, the *Gendarm*, insisted it could compete with any cake anywhere—my mother, with fingers trembling and her hair refusing to stay curled, announced her entry the week before Thanksgiving.

During the days leading up to the contest I stayed in school as long as I could, then went home with one friend or another. If Alex had to help at his father's inn and Christian was nowhere to be found, I followed Anke Hoffmann to her house and played all afternoon with her and Linde Janeke. Patiently I combed the hair of their dolls and listened to stories about cursed princes and princesses immortally in love with young men of low birth, only so Mrs. Hoffmann would invite me for dinner. All the dolls had names. Some were called only Dolly or Baby, but the better ones had names like Rosemarie and Kunigunde. Two of the dolls looked very similar, and both wore flowered dresses; they were Anke and Linde. The real girls almost looked like twins, and they often wore the same colors to heighten that impression. But Anke wore shiny barrettes and necklaces, and her shoes always looked freshly polished. Even her dolls looked more glamorous than Linde's, and she had twice as many as her friend and a whole drawer full of dresses for them. She insisted that her dolls wear fresh clothes daily.

I never mentioned those afternoons to Christian or Alex, and hoped the girls and Anke's brothers wouldn't tell on me. Yet each day I stayed as long as the Hoffmanns would have me. Only after nightfall did I return home, and neither my father nor my mother ever noticed my absence.

Each day my mom baked several small sheets of cake, trying to improve on the moistness of the dough, its texture, butteriness, or even the way to sprinkle it with sugar. If she noticed me at all in those days, it was only to put a plate with a large piece of *Butterkuchen* in front of me. "Try it, Martin," she'd say, but I couldn't enjoy the treat. One false expression on my face would bring her to tears; no praise would appease her.

My sister, Birgit, was thirteen, almost twice my age, and usually out with some boy or other. But now she was forced to help, which she did with a face so frightened and serious, with eyes so large and wide, she appeared to have seen a ghoul; one false move and they might pop out and roll under the cupboard.

My father followed my example and stayed away as much as possible. He preferred a drunken brawl, a burglary, or even assault to the murderous atmosphere that had befallen our home, where the kitchen light stayed on long after midnight. After hours I picked him up at Frick's, where his uniform bought him as many drinks as he needed. "Of course I complimented her," I heard him lament on one of these occasions. "That's what I'm supposed to do. If I don't tell her how delicious her cake is— every single time—she thinks I'm ungrateful. If I want cake, I have to encourage her."

Peter Brodersen, whose own wife would take part in the roast contest, put one of his big hands consolingly on my father's shoulder.

"It'll be okay," Jens Jensen, the old peat cutter, said.

"It won't," my father sighed. "Her cake is fine for us, but it's not Meier quality. When she loses, I won't eat anything but dry bread for weeks. Her honor, her confidence—she'll be humiliated, laughed at. She'll never be able to set foot in Meier's bakery again."

New people in Hemmersmoor were regarded with suspicion, and you stayed new until well after you'd lived in our village for twenty years, possibly forever. Our neighbor Bernd Fitschen, who arrived in Hemmersmoor when he was a toddler, and whose sparse hair was now white, and who had great-grandchildren my age, was still called "the foreign Bernd." He'd moved here from Groß Ostensen, a city twenty kilometers to the east.

New people were supposed to fit in and keep a low profile and not draw any attention to themselves. So Helga Vierksen's entry to both the stew and roast contest, in only her third year in Hemmersmoor, would normally have raised eyebrows. Not this year though; this year my mother's herculean task took center stage and left the quick tongues of Hemmersmoor little time for other topics.

The shadows around my mom's eyes grew wider and darker, and her expression changed from euphoria to hopelessness in a fraction of a second. Friday night, two days before the contest, I heard her cursing herself in the kitchen. "You couldn't stay, could you, you vain hag?" she asked. "How Heidrun, Bertha, and Gertrude—how the whole village will laugh at you!"

I stole myself away and learned how to braid Linde's hair. It was brown and heavy, and Anke showed me how to do it and laughed at me when I was done. The braids weren't the same length and looked silly. Linde said it wasn't so bad.

When the Hoffmanns finally sent me home, my mother's kitchen was still brightly lit. My father crept into my bed after midnight and whispered, "Martin, move over, and for heaven's sake don't go downstairs."

What had Hemmersmoor done to deserve such a sunny day? Our climate was as rainy and dreary as any, but I can't remember a single Thanksgiving ruined by dark clouds and showers. Unfailingly Sunday crept over the peat bog, and the sun drove us out of bed and into church. Starched shirts and ties and dresses that had not fit even the year before made mass uncomfortable, but by the time we were free to walk over to Frick's Inn everyone's mood was as mild as the September day. Only the owners of the Big House, which stood several kilometers outside our village, didn't make an appearance. For such a family, the spectacle of our contest was a disgrace, and the thought that the von Kamphoffs should sit next to us on the wooden benches was ridiculous.

At one o'clock, with faces red from beer and Bommerlunder, the men led the way into the square, where the women had set up the different contests. The priest stuck red ribbons on the jurors' lapels and blouses, and the fifteen men and women lined up for their right to the first taste. The rest of us awaited our turn to dig in. Anke and Linde stood with their parents; they were wearing white dresses, and their braids were wound around their heads in the same manner. They waved at me, and I almost ran over to them but stopped myself just in time, pretending not to have noticed them and hiding red-faced behind my father's broad back.

The jurors ladled stew into their bowls and slurped and smacked their lips while making important faces. They had been drawn lottery-style, to preclude any misgivings. If you judged the contest one year, you were not eligible for jury duty the next.

Hemmersmoor had experienced its scandals. Nine years before, a farmer's wife had bribed jurors and later been barred from the contest for life. Now Heidrun Brodersen's three-year winning streak was the subject of terrible suspicion by those who had tasted her roast at one of the Brodersens' dinners. Yet by and large the system had proved useful.

It came as a surprise then, when after half an hour of conscientious tasting, the newcomer Helga Vierksen's stew was awarded first prize. Yes, the jurors had to be fair, but they were indebted to tradition. Awarding Vierksen first prize was a slap in Hemmersmoor's face.

Even more surprising was that no one who had tasted her stew—with potatoes, carrots, and large, tender chunks of beef—protested. It seemed that even other contestants, among them staunch Hemmersmoor luminaries such as Rosemarie Penck, conceded defeat. Helga Vierksen's pots of stew spoke a clear language—only hers were empty, as though licked clean by hundreds of cats.

Helga, a large woman with large breasts and a fine smile with most of her teeth still intact, accepted the wooden plaque and said a simple thank-you. She knew not to gloat. Her five young children, the oldest being one of my classmates, stood around her, demanding to hold the prize. The crowd applauded hesitantly but with conviction. We weren't heartless.

The next contest produced Heidrun Brodersen's fourth consecutive victory, which had her neighbors shaking their heads. Yet on a sunny September afternoon, who wanted to argue?

My mother's face was so red when the final contest started, the skin stretched so tightly over her jaw, nose, and cheeks, I feared it might tear. All the while her false teeth kept grinning, with the gold wires of her dentures blinking in the light. Her twelve sheets of *Butterkuchen* outdid even the sun with their golden, buttery glow. The sugar sparkled.

And how we ate! We ate and ate, and sweat gathered on the fifteen jurors' brows and foreheads. The baker Meier, accepting the challenge, had exceeded our already high expectations, but had he surpassed my mother? His larger sheets seemed the only distinction between his cake and his competitor's.

So we ate more. We couldn't leave this matter to whimsy. Coffee was being served, thanks to Frick's generosity. All year he took what our fathers earned on the peat bog, but on Thanksgiving he gave back to everyone.

Around the time the jurors convened to decide on the winner, Jens Jensen, the old peat cutter, pointed at Otto Nubis and said, "Otto, your tongue is black."

"No, *yours* is as black as tar," Nubis, the foreman at Brümmer's tool factory, shot back.

When the priest approached them—sensing that a fistfight, another staple of our September feasts, might be at hand—and tried to calm them, the two men turned on him, grabbed him, and held open his jaw. "Your tongue is as black as your coat." And so it was. Soon we all stuck out our tongues, and they were black, every one of them. What had happened?

Our shock wore off soon. We knew this could have only one

explanation. Even though we hadn't experienced it ourselves, our history was clear on the matter: "For the first one death, for the second starvation, for the third one bread." We had eaten bread all our lives, but stories of our forebears and their plight lived on, and we knew what some of the first settlers on the Devil's Moor had done to save themselves from certain death. Now it had happened again. Our tongues were blackened because we had eaten human flesh.

Silence fell over the crowd, and all eyes searched for the contestants. My mother and the baker Meier did not come under suspicion, but where were the cooks of the roasts and stews?

"It's Heidrun," a voice cried. "That's why she wins every year." It was my father shouting. "I've eaten her roast, and it's no good."

"He's right," Bernd Fitschen cried. "It's Heidrun. That's why her roast is so tender."

The accused was a fat and charming woman, who turned the heads of Hemmersmoor's men. Her feet were stuck in the most fragile shoes I'd ever seen, and she was still holding on to her wooden plaque. "You ingrates," she shrieked. "I've lived with you all my life, and you're turning on me because your wives can't cook." Much of what she said after that was drowned out by cries to hack her to pieces. Until, in utmost despair, with a hundred hands grabbing her apron and dress, she shouted, "Why this time? You've eaten my roast before. It's not me."

While everyone was thinking about this, Heidrun took advantage of the break to continue. "It's not me. It's Helga. It's the new one."

Silence again. Hemmersmoor did not think fast on a full stomach. Yes, Heidrun's accusation made sense. Why else had Helga entered the contest but to poison us? Why else had we scraped her pots clean? Yes, Helga, the new one, was the culprit. People let go of Heidrun.

Her cries, her begging, her shrill voice didn't help Helga one bit and stopped no one, and when the village was done with her and her children, the bodies shapeless, resembling five small and one large bag filled with rags, sticks, and stones, my father led the way to Helga's house.

We set fire to home and barn. Helga's husband—having admitted his guilt by staying home—was struck down with an axe and dragged back into the house, where his remains were buried under falling beams and collapsing walls. The whole village watched and cheered the fire and helped a neighbor when flames from Helga's barn began licking his own.

After the pangs and the hissing had finally died down though, an eerie silence fell over the village. Our tongues were still black, but our rage had subsided. We stood around the still smoldering house like children, embarrassed, silent, but ready to attack anyone who would point a finger. The boys and girls of the village had screamed so much they had lost their voices and were now searching the ashes for little treasures. Anke and Linde stood to one side. They had pulled a badly singed hat with a colorful bow and a necklace with a green stone from Helga's house, and their white dresses were soiled and their braids hung limply at their sides.

That night Frick, against his custom, served a second round of free beer, and more bloodshed was avoided, even though many swore that next year it would be Heidrun's turn. Even when Jens Jensen claimed that Frick poured water into the beer, people answered with nothing but laughter.

The only person in Hemmersmoor who was not satisfied with Thanksgiving was my mother. No winner had been declared in the *Butterkuchen* contest, and the jurors, after acknowledging that their black tongues were in no shape to come to a sound judgment, refused to award first prize.

My dad welcomed the outcome. He was fond of pastries and did not want any misgivings between him and the baker. My mother, though, was not to be consoled.

When Anke and Linde asked me the following afternoon if I would come home with them to play, I answered in a loud voice, so Alex and the other boys could hear me, "I don't play with girls. I'm not stupid."

Christian

In the fall of Helga Vierksen's death, I was seven years old. She and her five children were clubbed to death in our village square, and their remains—what was left of them—were buried in a small lot in the cemetery outside the village. The cemetery was a windy affair, square and barren, and sometimes a few of us would approach it cautiously at night and watch little flames scurry over the graves.

That fall I should have been in school, but my parents had pleaded with the authorities, and it was agreed that I was to be given a year's reprieve. I wasn't allowed to be present during the talks, and I can't imagine what they hoped might change me during that one year. I had a lot of time on my hands, since Alex and Martin, my two loyal friends, were now learning math and reading and geography.

Just outside of Hemmersmoor stood Brümmer's tool factory. For reasons unknown, a huge window, not unlike a shop window, had been set into the wall just left of the office entrance. The factory had nothing to offer the villagers, nor did the villagers come to the factory to shop. About twenty men worked inside the cream-colored building, and none of them could say why the window had been inserted or who'd come up with the idea in the first place.

Even stranger was the setup of the window. It was impossible to peer into the office because on the inside a kind of alcove had been built, and a set of doors shut out our gazes from what lay beyond that alcove.

The sides, top, and bottom of the alcove were angled, lending a false perspective to the display, as though you were looking through a short tunnel or doorway. The most astonishing thing, however, lived inside the window. Otto Nubis, the foreman at Brümmer's, displayed his marionettes there, three or four at a time. This was not a gaudy display. The wooden people on the other side of the glass were not beautiful, their clothes shabby and discolored, their faces rough, serious, and more intimidating than the pictures of tortured saints in our church. They had a strange effect on my young mind: I feared them and yet couldn't keep myself from returning time and again.

The monotony of my days was interrupted during only two months. In March and October, in a sandy lot next to Frick's Inn, a small carnival set up its tents. We dreamt of Astro Blasters, the Galactic Loop, and the House of Primal Fear, but we were treated to shabby carousels and shooting stands where the BB guns were rusty and the barrels bent. Nobody ever won one of the five giant bears that dangled above those willing to pay.

While Alex and Martin were at school, I watched the carnies set up their tents. I knew the candy vendors and the mirrored maze, and I strolled past the groups of men and women who had fewer teeth and fingers than even the poorest peat cutters in Hemmersmoor.

One attraction I didn't recognize. The red-and-white tent

stood in back of the ship swings, and I saw a lanky man who looked old, but not in the way my parents did, standing in front, attaching a sign. "Ricos Reise Durch Die Hölle," it read: "Rico's Journey Through Hell." I stood and gaped.

"What's that?" I finally asked.

The man turned to face me. He wore a suit made from rough brown material, and his white shirt stood open at the neck. His skin was tough and wrinkled. He had a strong nose, a high forehead, and a chin with a deep cleft. Most impressive, though, were his eyes. They were watery and of such a light gray they seemed white. What could such eyes see? I wondered, and took two steps back.

"Who's asking?" the man said.

"I am," I said stubbornly.

The man, who I thought had to be Rico, laughed. "Do you have a name?"

"Christian Bobinski. Is that you?" I pointed to his sign. "What can I see in hell?"

"You can't wait, can you?" Rico said. "But hell isn't interested in you. You have to be eighteen to see my marvels."

"Rubbish," I said. "I'm old enough."

Rico laughed again. "Come tonight after midnight. If you do, and if you do me a favor, I will take you through hell."

Even at seven I knew that hell wasn't supposed to travel in a tent, and yet I couldn't find any rest throughout the day. I tied a tin can to my cat Melchior's tail and watched him take off in terror into the woods behind our garden. When my sister Ingrid, who was ten and in fourth grade, came home in the afternoon, I slipped a frog into her dress, and my parents promptly sent me to my room and locked the door. My eldest sister, Nicole, slid a note under my door. It read, "I hope they've thrown away the key."

Hell. What did Rico have to show me? I climbed through my window, jumped into the lime tree, and dropped to the ground. I had to find Alex and Martin.

They were at Alex's house. The teacher had told them to collect colorful leaves and dry them between sheets of blotting paper inserted into the pages of large and heavy books. Now they were trying the method on lizards and blindworms.

"Hell?" Martin asked. He was wiry and the tallest of us. His cropped hair and eyebrows were very red, his face full of freckles. He was the son of the *Gendarm*. "And he'll let you in?"

"If I do him a favor," I said.

Alex's lizard was still squirming, the tail twitching inside the *Brockhaus Encyclopedia*, volume A–D. Alex was Mr. Frick's son, and he was sturdily built and his eyebrows were bushy and growing together above his nose. His older brother, Olaf, should have inherited the inn, but he had no mind for working behind the bar and entertaining customers, and had moved out with his young wife. He was now working in Brümmer's tool factory.

Alex didn't concern himself with the family feud. He immediately moved into his brother's room. "What a fool," he said, whenever the grown-ups mentioned Olaf, and each and every time he did his father slapped his face. But the inn was his small kingdom. He knew how to get us food whenever we felt hungry. He'd stolen liquor from his father too.

"Is he the devil?" Alex asked.

"I don't know," I said. It didn't seem likely, yet his eyes had fascinated me. I had to get a pair of them.

At midnight I met my friends behind Frick's Inn. It was a Friday night, and the noise inside the pub would continue until the last drunk had been thrown out. There wasn't any rumor, any gossip that escaped Alex. Whatever secret the people of Hemmersmoor thought safe, alcohol finally dug it up and shouted it out, and in time Alex told Martin and me.

"It's the most amazing thing he's ever seen," he told us, about Jens Jensen, the peat cutter, who loved his Bommerlunder and who'd confessed many times to having sex with witches on the moor. "He saw the damned and their tortured souls, he says, and he says it could scare the devil himself."

The carnival had closed at midnight, and we were safe from the gazes of adults. Only the carnies were still milling around the tents, and they didn't look at us twice. What did they care about Hemmersmoor's children?

Rico's Journey Through Hell seemed to be deserted, the entrance locked, but after my third shout, Rico appeared from the darkness and smiled. "I didn't say you should bring them." He pointed at my friends. "Are you scared?" he asked me.

"I'm not scared," I said. "I want to see the souls."

"Of course you do," he answered. "But first you have to earn your journey through hell."

"How?" Alex said.

"Not you," Rico said. "Only this one here."

"That's not fair," Alex said. "I want to see hell too."

"You don't have anything I want," Rico told him. His eyes opened wider, their white color as sharp as steel. Alex shrank back.

"What do you want?" I asked.

Rico was tall, taller than my dad, taller than Jens Jensen. He was also thinner than anyone in Hemmersmoor. He still wore his brown suit, and I thought I could hear his bones clatter under the rough cloth.

"That's between the two of us," he said.

"We want to know," Martin insisted.

Rico looked at him for a second, and then, with a graceful bow, pulled off his right shoe. Alex and Martin ran. They abandoned me in front of Rico's Journey Through Hell. The air now smelled of sulfur, and Rico's eyes quieted down. He put his shoe back on, to conceal his hoof.

"You're not running?" he said.

"I want to see hell."

"I'll promise I'll show you. But first bring me the soul of your sister."

"How do I do that?"

Rico stooped and put a glass vial in my hand. "You steal into your sister's room and sit down on her bed. You say the words I'm going to tell you, and when her soul appears on her lips, you catch it for me." He pressed his lips to my ear and whispered the nine words it took to call the soul.

"Why didn't you want the souls of Alex's and Martin's sisters?" I asked before we parted.

"They are coarse. Their souls don't give any light. Your sister, now, she's different. Your sister's soul will shine."

"Young one," he called me back.

"Yes?"

"You have to do it tomorrow night. We'll meet here, and you shall see hell."

I feigned sickness the next day and stayed undisturbed in my room. In the afternoon Alex came to visit me. "What did he want?" he asked. He was ashamed of running off the night before. I could see it. But his curiosity was stronger.

"Where is Martin?" I asked him.

"He's at Anke's house. He plays with her and Linde's dolls," he sneered. "What a coward. He's a girl himself." He sneered once again. "So, what did Rico want?"

"Nothing," I said.

"Do you have to sell your soul?" Alex asked.

"No."

"He is the devil, isn't he?"

"Of course," I said.

"I knew it. I knew it. This morning Old Frieda found two of her roosters dead. They had turned black, inside and out, and she said it was a sign."

"Of course," I said again.

"And Jens Jensen was found in a ditch, unconscious, and he claimed he'd fought with the devil, who'd come to take him."

"Of course," I repeated.

"They're trying to shut Rico's tent down, but some say they won't take it up with the devil. They say they won't touch him."

"They won't," I said.

They didn't. Rico's tent stayed open, and everyone went to see hell's wonders. As for me, I waited until Ingrid had gone to bed. At eleven I stood by her side. Cautiously I leaned over her face and listened to her breathing. Her eyelids fluttered from time to time, but she remained silent. I took my mother's empty laundry bag

27

and pulled it slowly over Ingrid's face. Then I felt for her nose, pinched it shut and put my hand over her mouth. Ingrid awoke with a start and froze for a moment. Then she thrashed about. Her legs kicked out, her fingers tore into my face and scratched my cheeks. Ingrid pulled my hair and punched my nose. She twisted and turned, and I sat down on her chest and wouldn't let her escape. Her body jerked a few times, then her fingers fell away and she lay motionless in her bed. I pulled the bag, which was made from oilskin, off her face and tied it carefully shut. Whatever it was Rico wanted from me, I had caught it in this bag.

My sister's eyes stood open, but they remained without expression, dark, and without the faintest shimmer. I put an ear over her mouth, smoothed out her hair, and pulled the comforter over her body. But her right leg stuck out from underneath, and her foot seemed icy and green like spoiled milk. I took her big toe between my lips and sucked on it. Then I also stuffed her other toes into my mouth. I stuck my head under the comforter and under Ingrid's nightgown. I lay on top of her body, as though I could warm her, put my head on her breast and kissed her neck. Nothing seemed enough.

When it was time to leave, I stuffed the laundry bag under my jacket and hurried out of the room. Then I climbed once again through my window and into the garden, full of fear that I might lose Ingrid's soul.

Rico awaited me behind his tent. "Yes, you have come back. I knew," he said.

"Of course," I said.

"You caught it," he said, but it sounded like a question.

"Of course." I patted my pants' pocket, in which I carried the empty vial. "Now show me everything."

"I want to see it," he demanded.

"Later," I said.

He nodded, but couldn't take his eyes off me. Then he shook his head and pushed open the entrance.

The walls were covered with paintings of the different chambers of hell. In one you could see sinners being stripped of their colorful clothes and pushed into vats of hot oil. Another picture showed naked sinners being cut open by hordes of devils and being hung from sharp hooks and roasted above great fires.

"Are you scared?" Rico asked.

"No," I said. "Show me."

He led me to several shelves of vials just like the one he had given me to capture Ingrid's soul. They shone faintly in the relative dark of the tent. "These I keep before I toss them into my eternal flames," Rico whispered hoarsely.

"What else have you got?" I asked.

Rico led me to a heap of bones, the remains of sinners who had died in hell's fires. The bones were charred, blackened.

"What else?"

He took me into the farthest corner of his tent. "Here," he said. "You can look directly into hell." He pulled the large black cloth off a barrel and had me look inside. "It sits right above hell's entrance," Rico said. "Hell's entrance is in Hemmersmoor."

Fog and steam rose from the barrel, and as soon as I pushed my face over its opening, I could hear voices coming from deep below. The voices were mourning, lamenting their deaths, screaming in agony. "That's hell," Rico said. "Now you've seen it."

"Yes," I answered.

"I kept my promise," he said. He flipped a switch and hell

stopped moaning. No more steam rose from the barrel. The glass vials on the shelves stopped flickering.

"I kept mine." I pulled the glass vial out of my pocket and handed it to him.

He stared at it intently. "It's empty," he said. "Didn't you use the nine words I gave you?" His voice was coarse.

"Of course not." I unbuttoned my jacket and handed him the laundry bag. "Words are not enough."

His hands started to shake when he took the bag from me. "What is this?" he asked. Slowly he began to untie it.

The sky was hung with stars, the air, after Rico's sulfuric tent, dewy and calming. Fall had retained a hint of warmth, and I walked home at a leisurely pace and without any disturbance. Shouting and angry voices came from Frick's Inn, not unlike the noise that had emanated from Rico's hell.

I climbed up the lime tree and jumped onto my windowsill. The house was quiet, my parents asleep. My bed was damp and cold to the touch.

They found Ingrid early the next morning, when they tried to wake her for church and couldn't. For the rest of the day, our house was filled with visitors, mourners, and relatives. I was put in a black suit and wasn't allowed to leave the house or attend the funeral the following week.

Linde

I cannot remember my father's hands without dirt under his nails. He was a small, wiry man with a shiny scalp that he protected with a handkerchief in the summer. My parents' marriage was not happy, largely because he never made much money from keeping the grounds at the von Kamphoffs' manor. Our house was a rickety one-story affair with hardly enough yard space for a few flowers.

"At least they could have put you up at the Big House," my mother, Therese, said so often that my dad and I would finish that sentence aloud for her. This, I see now, could have been a moment of harmony, one in which he could have acknowledged his shortcomings as a provider, and she her futile aspirations. They could have laughed at themselves. Yet my mom's face grew so hard at our antics that the lightest touch would have caused it to crack and fall away. It was the end of any conversation, any meal, any warmth.

Of my earliest trips to the Big House, I remember next to nothing, but after I turned four I spent every summer with my father, and every morning I ran along the hedges and bushes and inhaled the strangely heavy scent of the still-closed blossoms. Even though I wasn't technically allowed to wander the grounds, the von Kamphoffs liked my father well enough not to say a word. They knew that no one else would have done so much work for so little.

When I turned seven, however, I had to braid my hair and attend school, and let Dad do his work without my good cheer and companionship. Instead of lending him a hand, I sat in the classroom, next to my best friend, Anke Hoffmann, and learned how to write and do math. I felt very important with my new books and my large schoolbag, and instead of collecting acorns or raking leaves I spent my afternoons at Anke's house. I spent so much time with her that I started to feel like a stranger in my own home.

The winter after I started school was no winter at all. In the fall Martin Schürholz had often played with Anke and me, but since our Thanksgiving celebration his visits had become less frequent. When he came to Anke's room, it was only to braid our hair and put his face in our laps. Or we played wedding, and he was the groom and had to kiss us.

The Vierksen family had been buried on a sunny September day, and at the end of October the sun still made us sweat when we went in our black dresses to Ingrid Bobinski's funeral. Then the November storms never came, and even on the first Sunday in Advent the windows of our houses were still open and the candles on the pine wreaths put no one in a festive mood. The boys in our village met at night to go swimming in the Droste River.

That December the villagers got quickly used to the warm weather, but when it was almost Christmas and they still hadn't rummaged through the dark corners of their closets to retrieve their mothballed winter coats, they started to get worried. They enjoyed the mild days and even tolerated the flies, which sat on their doors and windows and crept into their bedrooms and hummed around their sleeping babies, but how long could such a blessing last? Winter had to come after all. It had to snow; the canals had to freeze over. The warmer the days got, the more worried the farmers became. Had Helga Vierksen put a curse on Hemmersmoor? Was it time to pay for our sins? The trees blossomed, grass and grains started to push out of the soil—a sudden frost would cost them their harvest. My father shook his head and sighed. In winter he often came home early; the gardens could do without him. Yet the warm weather would not allow him to rest.

The only woman in the village wearing her black coat was the widow Madelung. She wore black all year, and it was her only coat. Even though the woolen fabric had to be too warm, she wore the coat whenever she left the von Kamphoff manor to walk into the village.

After the last war, the administration in Groß Ostensen had insisted that the von Kamphoff family take in war refugees. This was how Inge Madelung and her young son, Friedrich, came to live in a tiny room at the Big House. She was a small woman, with white, curly hair that, it was said, on the evening before her escape from East Prussia had still been flaxen. Inge Madelung wasn't yet forty years old, and even though her face looked tired and drawn, she was met with suspicion by the women in Hemmersmoor whenever she came to buy a few things for herself and her son. She didn't have a husband, she held herself straight, and she had kept her youthful figure.

Hermann Madelung, who had worked as a waiter before the

war, had never come home from the Lithuanian front, Mrs. Meier told her patrons. As long as his death wasn't established, the small woman would not receive a pension. What a cruel fate, sighed Mrs. Meier, and the women in the bakery sighed with her a bit too heartily.

In the summer Inge Madelung worked in the fields around the Big House, and in the fall and winter she did the laundry and helped in the kitchen. She was a good worker, diligent, conscientious, and quiet.

Friedrich grew and started going to school in the village. He was needled because of his mended shirts and socks. He always wore the same pair of pants—clean, mended at the knees, and a bit shabbier every month—until he was finally too tall for them.

Friedrich often bragged about his father, told stories of his daring adventures in the last war. One day his father flew in an attack on Moscow, on another he saved his men by jumping out of a trench and storming toward the enemy all by himself. He'd been a high-ranking officer, Friedrich told us, and had received many medals. Friedrich was the only one in our class whose father wasn't around, and his stories grew ever more fantastic. But Alex and Bernhard called him a bastard, and he often went home from school crying after fighting with Martin and the others. Rumors were flying that neither Friedrich nor his mother knew who the boy's father was. She had been too friendly with soldiers or maybe something much worse had happened, something the women in Hemmersmoor never named. They said Inge should be happy that her son didn't look like a Mongol or a Moor.

Inge Madelung, however, ignored these rumors and mended her son's pants after every fight. When she came into the village, she held her head high, even though the other women's hostility was palpable and can't have escaped her. They worried about their men, called her the Crow behind her back, but loudly enough so she could hear it. She never came to our Thanksgiving celebrations.

No matter how much Inge wished for a friendlier reception in Hemmersmoor, she understood the women's hostility all too well. She felt the men's stares like needles on her skin, and was treated without any respect by them, as though she had personally caused her husband's death.

All that would probably have escaped me—Anke and I had better things to do than to worry about the adults' affairs—if my father had stayed home like every other winter, if his hedges and flower beds had been buried under a thick layer of snow. But the old owner insisted that my dad work long hours in the gardens of the Big House, and the strangest thing was that it didn't seem to bother my father. Quite the opposite. Each morning he seemed to get up a little bit earlier than the previous one, and my mother started to complain about his early rising, his good spirits, and loud voice. When my father returned home in the evenings, she was in such a foul mood that I left the house to make Christmas decorations from colored paper and straw with Anke.

What I didn't know, but what my mom told me all too soon in a low whisper, was that Inge Madelung was helping my dad with his work. In the fall Inge had helped in the fields, just like the previous year, but one day the overseer had approached her and asked if she would like to help the gardener with his work. Inge had agreed and had been happy to escape the sun beating down on her without respite. My father had shaken his head when the overseer introduced him to Inge, had complained to my mother that she couldn't lift and carry like a man.

But after the first week, he had been surprisingly satisfied with her work, and after another week, they could often be seen working side by side until my father drove home at night in his beat-up truck.

My mother's face was dark, her eyes shimmered, and something that appeared to be a smile, but was so much more dangerous, played on her lips while she told me all this two days before our Christmas recess. "The worst," she said, "is that he won't talk about her at all anymore. He's keeping her a secret. He can't wait to be alone with that hussy. Your father is not himself anymore. He's long forgotten about the two of us."

I didn't answer my mother. No word could have consoled her or changed the plan she had come up with. As soon as school let out for Christmas, I was to accompany my dad to the Big House again. "You have to keep your eyes open and tell me everything you see," she said.

"Can Anke come with me?" I asked.

My mom nodded. "Just don't let on."

On December 21, at five o'clock in the morning, my dad and I left the house and picked up Anke, who was already waiting outside her house, freshly washed and groomed. Together we trundled through the darkness toward the Big House.

Anke carried a small leather bag that her mother had packed for her, and she stared intently through the side window. She wore a dress, which was, unlike my own, much too nice to wear for work or play, and she looked all pretty and smelled as if her mom had rubbed her whole body with cologne. "Can we go into the maze?" she asked.

"As long as you don't get caught," mumbled my father. Last summer my presence had still cheered him up, but this winter morning he was moody. "Don't do anything foolish and, above all, be courteous to old man von Kamphoff. Curtsy when you see him."

Three generations of the von Kamphoff family lived in the manor house. The old owner had served as an officer in two wars. He was missing an arm and had a pronounced limp. It was he who had first hired my dad, when my father was a young man with a pregnant bride, and he treated Dad with the same benevolence one might show to a favorite dog. His legs were white and crisscrossed by varicose veins and scars, and one shirtsleeve was rolled up and fastened to the shoulder with safety pins.

Some days he stood next to my dad, who was digging up weed trees or planting rhododendrons, and rambled on good-humoredly about the battles he'd fought in. He explained why we should have won the wars and which mistakes and coincidences had prevented us from claiming what was destined to be ours.

My father agreed. He might have been a good, gentle man, but if his bad eyes had not kept him out of the service, he would readily have fought for the *Vaterland*. He was poor, Hemmersmoor was poor, someone had to be responsible for the misery in the world, and it couldn't be us. Not us.

Only a few people in the village had ever visited the manor, and even fewer had set foot inside. Yet this fact added spice to the rumors that swirled around the von Kamphoff family. It was said that the old Johann von Kamphoff had murdered his father in his sleep to become lord of the manor, and that a black woman he had captured during the last war was imprisoned in the basement. The patrons of Frick's Inn again and again talked about the true heir. They claimed that Johann had had a younger brother, and that this brother, against all customs, should have inherited the manor. But after the death of his father, Johann hadn't wanted to cede what he thought was his and had killed his brother. In a different version of the story, Johann had imprisoned his brother, just like the black woman. Yet nobody could remember what the true heir had looked like. All this had happened before the first of the wars, and birth certificates weren't archived in Hemmersmoor.

Today, though, it wasn't old von Kamphoff who greeted us when we arrived at the manor house. It was Inge Madelung, and as soon as my dad had climbed out of his truck, he introduced us to her. "Winter recess," he mumbled. "They're in the way at home."

Inge shook hands with us as though we were already grown up. "You must be going to school with my Friedrich," she said.

"Yes," Anke said. "He's in our class."

"How nice," said the widow. "Maybe you'd like to play together."

"Maybe," I said without enthusiasm, but my dad looked sternly in my direction, then sent me and Anke to get rakes, garden shears, and buckets from the toolshed. "You can give us a hand," he said, and soon we were pulling weeds and raking the lawn.

"This is stupid," Anke said. Her hands were already covered in blisters. "My mom is baking cookies today."

I stuck my tongue out and said, "Why don't you run home?"

"And later we have to play with that bastard," she complained.

"Yeah, that's really stupid," I agreed. I couldn't tell her the true reason why we had come to the manor. My mom had forbidden me to make a single peep, but her admonishment hadn't been necessary. "When the old man joins us, we can go and play." I tried to appease her.

Last summer Mr. von Kamphoff had come into the garden two, maybe three, times a week, but now my dad was complaining about his constant presence. "Here he comes again," he said under his breath when, around nine o'clock, the old owner made his way toward us. He seemed to abhor the many visits his employer made, and I noticed that Johann von Kamphoff's appearance had changed. His hair was neatly cut and glistened with grease. He had stopped wearing his worn and shapeless pants, and his shoes had been shined. He greeted me and Anke, and we both curtsied; then he turned to the widow and asked, "Mrs. Madelung, busy again?"

"Let's go," I whispered into Anke's ear, but my friend shook her head silently.

"What's the matter?" I asked, but I still didn't receive an answer. Instead Anke stared at the old man, and whenever he looked in her direction, she smiled diligently. Finally she stooped and pretended to pull weeds while listening intently to the adults' conversation.

While Johann von Kamphoff was talking about his war adventures, my father's face grew increasingly somber. "Didn't have to kill them," the owner sighed. "Could have simply disowned them." He still wore his shirtsleeve rolled up and pinned to the shoulder, but the shirt was made from silk, and he wore an expensive tie.

"Absolutely," my father agreed. "Would have been better for the war effort."

"Damn mess," cursed Mr. von Kamphoff, and then looked

at Inge, who quickly turned away and pretended not to have overheard the men's conversation.

"Erich," the owner said, and pointed to my father. "Erich thinks he's the only one who knows anything about garden work." He laughed jovially. "But I wasn't always a silly old man. I traveled the world. Saw Africa, the desert, the Muslims, the black devils. A fascinating continent."

Even I was listening to the old man now, just like Anke. Maybe the black woman in the basement wasn't just a rumor after all. Maybe the people in the village had been right all along.

Inge smiled. "How are your grandchildren doing?" she asked. "My Fritz worships your Rutger."

Anke's face lit up as soon as the widow mentioned Rutger von Kamphoff. The owner's grandson had to be thirteen or fourteen, and all my friends wanted to marry him. He didn't go to school in Hemmersmoor, but from time to time a black Mercedes appeared in our village, and when the von Kamphoff family stepped out onto our cobblestone streets, the villagers dropped whatever they were doing and stared open-mouthed at the spectacle. After each and every of Rutger's visits, all the girls claimed he had winked at them.

Yet the old man didn't seem to have heard the question. "It's a shame that a young woman like you has to fend for herself," he said. "Your husband was a soldier?"

Inge nodded. "He died in Lithuania."

Johann von Kamphoff grunted. "A shame," he said. "I think I might be able to help you out a bit. Is there anything you need? Does your son need anything? I don't want to embarrass you, but if you're missing something, please let me know." His face had been unusually grim during his little speech, but now it lit up again. "We have to help one another, right?" he said. "You are a wonderful worker. I'm not offering any handouts."

Inge nodded. She didn't know what to say to all this. "Thank you," she squeezed out and smiled. The old man smiled back, winked at her, and quickly turned away.

My father's voice became audible again only after the heat had driven Johann von Kamphoff back to the manor house. "You can't work like this," he moaned. "Yes, Mr. von Kamphoff. Absolutely right, Mr. von Kamphoff." For a while he stared ahead, lost in thought; then he turned on Inge. "And all this because of you. Smile, make a pretty face. Encourage that old goat. You'll see what it gets you." Anger colored his face purple.

Inge stayed silent and quickly looked at me and Anke; she hadn't forgotten about our presence. "Should I return to the fields?" she asked quietly.

Now my father turned to look at us. "Nonsense," he exclaimed quickly, and his anger subsided momentarily.

Around noon Friedrich stepped into the garden to bring his mother sandwiches and an apple. He looked at Anke and me as though we were apparitions, and then frowned. My father took our lunch from the truck, handed me the sandwiches my mother had wrapped in coarse paper, and said, "Go ahead. You can show Friedrich the maze. But don't yell and scream. Nobody has to know you're in there."

Only slowly did we leave our parents. Friedrich seemed displeased by the idea of having us around. He stopped and turned to look at his mom time and again, but she waved him away. Scowling, he followed Anke and me through the garden. "I already know the maze," he said. "It's boring."

"You're boring," Anke shot back.

"Why do you want to go to the maze?" he asked. "The hedges are all bare."

"Anke has never been there. It's her first time at the manor," I said importantly.

"I know it inside and out," he said quickly. "And I'm allowed to go to the stables whenever I want. Maybe they'll let me ride one of the horses sometime soon."

"They don't belong to you," Anke said. "You don't belong here."

"So?" Friedrich said. "Without Linde, you wouldn't be here. And she's only the gardener's daughter."

"And she isn't allowed to ride the horses either."

"But I'm a boy." Friedrich blocked Anke's path. "Why are you so dolled up?"

"Because my mom won't let me run around in old rags," she quipped, but Friedrich had already shoved her to the ground. "Dumb cow," he said.

I knew what I owed my friend and slapped Friedrich hard in the face. I thought he would hit me back, but he only looked at me for a moment, then turned and ran away. "Friedrich," I called after him—I feared my dad would be angry if he found out what happened—but he didn't come back.

When it was time to return home, it stayed very quiet in our truck. My dad turned to gaze at me from time to time but didn't say a word. Anke's dress was soiled, and I could feel that she regretted ever having agreed to come. She could have baked cookies with her mother; now she had blisters on her hands, hadn't found the maze to her taste, hadn't seen any horses, and, worst of all, hadn't caught a single glimpse of Rutger von Kamphoff.

"Thank you, Mr. Janeke," she said nicely and icily in front of her house. "You want to come over tomorrow?" she asked me while she was climbing out of the truck. "My dad is going to decorate the tree with us."

"You go," my father said. "I'll be okay on my own." But I shook my head. I had given my word.

That evening my mother took me aside and questioned me about Inge Madelung. How was she dressed? What did she talk about with my dad? Was she really constantly at his side? What had she said and done?

I loved my father, but I feared my mother. I had to give her something if I wanted to stay in her good graces.

"The owner of the manor seems to like her well," I said, and told her about the old man's peculiar behavior.

"It's a shame," she said. "What a cunning person. Well, she doesn't own a thing, so she has to go after our men." But no matter how much she cursed and complained, the news seemed to please her. She praised my effort, tousled my hair, and stroked my cheeks. "Be nice to Friedrich," she said. "See if he tells you something."

Later that evening my dad called me and asked if I had made friends with Friedrich. I confessed what had happened, and what Anke had said, and he nodded. Finally he said, "It's not as easy for Friedrich as it is for you girls."

"But he's dumb and stupid," I said.

"He's only afraid."

"Afraid of us?"

"He's not from here, and you let him feel that." He paused a moment. "Do you really want to come with me again tomorrow morning?"

"Yes," I said. "Do the von Kamphoffs really have a black woman in the basement?"

My father looked at me in surprise; he'd never been interested in rumors. "Maybe you and Friedrich can find out tomorrow," he laughed. Then his face was all serious again. "Don't tell your mother anything about Mrs. Madelung. It will only upset her."

I nodded.

"She doesn't understand the work I'm doing, how good it feels to have someone who is meticulous, hardworking, and who you can count on. Your mother sometimes suspects the worst things imaginable, but we know better, don't we?" he asked.

I nodded again.

"And be nice to Friedrich. Maybe you can still become friends," he said slowly. "Are you still playing with your model train?"

The next morning, while my mom was boiling water for his coffee, my dad came to my room, and with my help, he snuck out of the house for a few short minutes without my mother noticing. When we reached the manor house in our three-wheeled truck and Inge Madelung came to greet us, he took a large wooden box from its bed. "It's nothing," he explained. "Only old toys Linde has no use for anymore." And as an answer to Inge's surprised look, he quickly added, "She never owned any dolls." His face turned red and he grinned sheepishly. "I guess I always wanted . . ." He stopped himself. "I can help you carry all that junk home."

"I can handle it," Inge protested, but my dad would have none of it.

"It's pretty heavy," he said. "Really is."

I followed the adults, and when we came to Inge's doorstep, they suddenly grew eerily quiet. I remember how embarrassed my father seemed. With that big box of his, he stood in front of Inge's door and large drops were visible on his forehead, but it is clear to me now that he wasn't sweating because of the unusually warm weather. I still see Inge's hand around the doorknob, hesitating, unable to make a move. But Friedrich had heard us come and finally opened the door from the inside and let us in. His face looked grim. We must have been the first visitors in the two years since they had come to Hemmersmoor.

"Just put it down somewhere," Inge said to my father. "I'll take care of it later. Thank you so much."

My dad didn't leave immediately though. He set down the box and slowly looked around Inge's chamber. "A bit tight," he said. "They couldn't find anything smaller for you, right? But it's clean, everything's shipshape." He nodded. "It's a lot of toys."

"What do you say?" Inge asked her son.

"Thank you," Friedrich said.

"Thank you so much," Inge said and started toward the door.

"Yes, we should get to work," Dad said. But he took another moment to inspect the room. "No photo of your husband?" he suddenly asked.

Inge blushed. "I lost everything," she quickly answered.

"That's right," Dad said. "Well, we should really go. Maybe Linde can help Friedrich put everything together?"

"Well, yes, but . . . ," Inge said slowly, turning around to look at her son.

"But shouldn't I help you outside?" I pleaded.

"We'll be okay without you," my dad answered.

"But if she'd rather help?" Inge said.

"We'll be fine," he said brusquely, and a few minutes later I found myself alone with Friedrich in that small room. He stood in front of the large box, obviously curious about what was inside but too proud to make a move.

"Anke isn't here," I said into the silence. I remembered my mother's instructions: I had to befriend the boy.

"She's stupid," he said.

"Not at all," I shot back. "Maybe a little."

"You are nicer," he said matter-of-factly, and then we unpacked the toys together, assembled the tracks, and cleaned the railroad cars. "And you really don't want them anymore?" he asked.

I shrugged my shoulders. "My mother says I'm too old for such things."

"I'm just as old as you are."

"But you're a boy," I said.

He looked at me in puzzlement, then stared at the steam engine in his hand and said, "I think your dad likes my mom."

I paused a moment in horror. Until now this whole affair had been a complicated game between my parents, but to hear those words from Friedrich's mouth made it all real. He was right, there could be no doubt. "Don't be silly," I said.

"See for yourself." He stood up and ran over to a dresser, pulled open a drawer, and showed me its contents. "He always brings her things, even when she doesn't want them." Inside the drawer was a small clay vase, which I had made for my father at school, and next to it a necklace with a blue pendant. A crocheted handkerchief, a bar of soap that smelled of roses, a pin cushion. "Almost every day he gives her something." Friedrich's tone of voice balanced between accusatory and confidential. "She thinks she's keeping it secret, but lately she's behaved so differently."

"Different how?"

"Yesterday she hit me because I came home with my clothes dirty. And then she immediately started to cry. I tried to console her, but she wept all night. And this morning she slapped me because I wasn't ready on time."

"You're lying," I said. "That's a lie. Your mother is an evil woman."

"Take that back," he said.

"Don't hold your breath," I replied. "Mom is right—your mother is bad." I slapped his face.

Yet this time Friedrich did not run away. He hit my face and tears came to my eyes; I pulled his hair. He screamed, grabbed my dress. Then he bit my arm, and I stepped on his toes and pushed him. Friedrich stumbled and fell, landing on the postal car. Maybe we would have bloodied each other, but at that moment we heard steps outside the front door, and Friedrich jumped to his feet. "If you tell on me, you're dead," he whispered.

A moment later Inge Madelung opened the door, and behind her appeared the old owner of the manor with his immaculately shined shoes. "Wouldn't it be great? There's nothing like a brisk ride across the moor." He laughed and raised his left hand in a fist.

"Friedrich?" Inge said. "I hope you don't mind the mess. Mr. Janeke—"

"Nonsense," said Johann von Kamphoff, stepping carefully over the tracks and engines. "I really don't want to bother you and keep you away from the garden, but I'd like to know if you have everything you need."

Inge, Friedrich, and I stayed silent and watched the owner unabashedly inspect the small room. And didn't it all belong to him? It was his property, his own house. He walked about, put a finger to his mouth, then swished it along the high edge of a small wardrobe. "Ah," he exclaimed. "What a woman. Perhaps I should have you work in the Big House. All that hard work in the gardens must wear you out. And Janeke is a crank. He's no companion for someone like you, Mrs. Madelung."

Mortified, I cast down my eyes. The old owner turned to Friedrich. "Hello, young man," he said with a smile. "Does your mom take good care of you? She's telling me that you resemble your dad very much. Is that right?" He turned to Inge and winked at her before addressing the boy once more. "We will find some better rooms for you and your mom. A man like you needs a bit of space, right? A good desk to study at too. You shouldn't grow up in such a tiny box."

Friedrich nodded quietly. Inge went to stand behind him, as though she needed to protect her son. She seemed very small, and her voice was barely audible. "Thank you very much, Mr. von Kamphoff," she said. "But you have done enough."

"Nonsense," he said, and slowly walked toward the front door. "You are a formidable mother. Those weren't empty words.

Next week we will furnish you with a better room." He was silent for a moment, then looked at her with a serious expression. Slowly he nodded his head. "This weather, this weather . . ." Before leaving, he touched her cheek and caressed it. "Nature is sometimes odd."

On Christmas it rained all day and night, yet it was so warm that the people in Hemmersmoor opened their windows anyway and took long walks in shirtsleeves and rubber boots. The star singers carried umbrellas, and the water in the canals rose and flooded the bogs. The Christmas trees seemed out of place; the gingerbread cookies softened and wouldn't taste right.

Mom remained suspicious of my dad, and my report about Johann von Kamphoff's visit to the widow's chamber only confirmed her opinion about Inge Madelung. I kept quiet, however, about what Friedrich had showed me; I was too afraid of the consequences. The warm weather couldn't soothe her, and on Christmas Eve my mother argued with my dad. She felt he didn't tell her everything, and what she suspected must have been even worse than the truth. "I can't believe you're not at the manor tonight," she said after dinner. "You and the Crow are so close these days. I don't understand why you come home at all."

My father lowered his head and didn't answer. We could hear how he slowly exhaled. His head and neck turned red.

"She hasn't changed, that bitch. First she lets some soldier get her pregnant, and now she's trying to steal my man."

My father jolted upright. His face was glum and he shook his fists, but no words came from his half-open mouth. He blew out the candles on the Christmas tree, took his hat and coat, and returned only after midnight. I had to unwrap my presents alone in my room.

The holidays were even worse, and the atmosphere so poisonous that on the morning of December 26, I went to Anke's to play with her new dolls. She was the Hoffmanns' only daughter, and her mother showered her with gifts, all of which she showed me the second I stepped into the house. Instead of playing in the living room as usual, we sat on a bench in the garden, placing the dolls on chairs around us. It was so warm that the boys ran through the village in shorts and without shoes. After the previous day's rain, the streets were soft and muddy, and there were large puddles all over the village square. Mr. Frick had carried chairs outside, and the men were drinking their beer under the oak trees, their collars open.

"My mother is going to Groß Ostensen the day after tomorrow," Anke told me. "She wants to buy fabrics. You want to come with us?"

"Yes," I said immediately, but then thought better of it. "Another time. I have to help my dad."

Anke rolled her eyes. "Do you have to play with Friedrich again?"

I shrugged. "He doesn't have anybody else to play with during recess."

"Serves him right. My mother says he needs a father. But of course that's not going to happen." She tapped her forehead. "Where would he get one?"

Only in the late afternoon, after the sun went down, did I return home. My dad was nowhere to be seen, but my mom had visitors. When I stepped into the lighted kitchen, Mrs. Meier, the baker's wife; Mrs. Schürholz, the *Gendarm*'s wife; and the mailman's wife were sitting around the table. This was no coffee klatch, however. A marble cake stood between them, but my mom hadn't used the good china; the women drank their coffee from the plain blue-and-white cups.

They fell silent while my mother piled the rest of our Christmas dinner onto my plate and sent me to my room. Once there I closed my door from the outside, but loud enough for the women to notice, then put down my plate and listened to their voices from an armchair in our living room. They sounded very serious and secretive, so I couldn't overhear much, but I heard the word "crow" several times, and when the women finally said good night, Mrs. Schürholz reassured my mom, "Klaus can get you the forms. We'll deal with that in the New Year. You'll see." And the mailman's wife said, "My husband can arrange that. He'll deliver it personally."

"You should have come to us earlier," Mrs. Meier said. "No need to be ashamed."

My dad seemed relieved when the holidays were over. His face smoothed out for the first time in three days, and the closer we got to the manor, the brighter his eyes shone from behind his thick glasses.

But Inge did not join us in the garden; instead Friedrich came running. "She has a fever and is sleeping." He himself looked all gray.

My dad listened to him and nodded. "That's fine. Tell her to rest." Then he paused before asking, "Does she need any medication? Shall I get the doctor for her?" He took a few steps toward the manor house, but then stopped. "Linde," he instructed me. "You go and see if Mrs. Madelung needs anything."

"You don't need to come," Friedrich said once we were out of earshot. "It's not a real fever."

"Not a real fever?"

"Well, she's sick, but in a different way." When I looked at him without comprehending, he added, "She hasn't slept all night. I think she saw my dad."

"But he's dead," I said out loud, and then put my hand quickly over my mouth.

He shrugged. "She really saw him though, I think." And then Friedrich told me what had happened. His mom had given him a new pair of pants for Christmas, and against her wishes he had worn them to play outside. But after hanging around the stables, he had slipped on a muddy path and torn a big hole in the left knee. He hadn't dared go home for a long time, and when he finally returned, after dark, Inge struck him repeatedly. But still her rage wouldn't subside, and she scolded him, called him an ungrateful brat who only caused her pain. She paced her room, up and down, and up and down, and cursed her fate, cursed the death of her husband, cursed Hemmersmoor and old Mr. von Kamphoff. "And your dad as well," Friedrich added. "She was beside herself, and then she started to cry and got only more furious, until she finally ran outside."

The night air was damp but hadn't cooled off. On her way into the gardens, Inge had not once looked over her shoulder, and Friedrich had hurried from bush to bush and followed her at a safe distance. Near the parkway that led to the road to Hemmersmoor, where you could no longer see the lights from the manor house, Inge had stopped. "She was yelling at my father," Friedrich said. "'Hermann,' she was yelling, again and again. And then she said that he was to blame for all her misery. That he had been only a stupid waiter, and that he had left us voluntarily to go to war. He had been nothing more than canon fodder and left us without money or help, and she had had to escape without him."

His mother had cried loudly and finally she had shouted, "Hermann! Where are you? What have you done to me, Hermann? What were you doing on the battlefield? You couldn't even shoot properly. How could you be so dumb and die in a foreign country? What is going to happen to me? To your son? Come back, Hermann, come and help me. It's all your fault. Come and help me!"

Friedrich was too afraid to leave his hiding place. He was afraid for his mother, but he feared her wrath even more. Yet he kept watching her and suddenly became aware of a white figure among the trees along the parkway. It seemed to scurry from tree to tree without ever touching the ground. "Hermann?" Inge asked, and when the white figure approached her, she screamed, "Hermann!" and began to cry. "Forgive me. I didn't want to wake you. Go back, Hermann, go back to sleep. I will manage on my own. Forgive me, Hermann, I will let you sleep. I won't cry anymore, Hermann."

What had happened afterward, Friedrich couldn't say. "I ran away," he said quietly and without looking at me. With the tips of his shoes, he was drawing lines into the sand.

"Was it really your dad?" I asked.

He shrugged his shoulders. "I didn't imagine all this."

"Maybe it was one of the von Kamphoffs," I suggested. "Or

maybe Johann's brother, the true heir. Maybe he escaped from the basement."

"Those are old wives' tales," said Friedrich.

"They're not," I insisted.

"In any case don't tell my mother I told you," he admonished me. "Don't let on."

Together we stepped into their room. Mrs. Madelung slept and didn't awaken when we tiptoed to her bed and made sure that her eyes were closed and that she was breathing regularly. Her cheeks looked all red, and her wrinkles had smoothed out. From time to time she snored a little.

Friedrich pulled me back and cautiously opened a drawer and took out a photograph, which he showed me once we got outside. "It's the only one we have," he said, and let me hold it. It showed a man with thinning hair, wearing a dark suit. He had a fine smile and large, dark eyes. The edges and corners of the picture were bent and worn.

"Was he an officer?" I asked.

Friedrich shook his head. He blushed and said, "I lied."

"How did he die, then?"

"We don't know," he said. "And my mother never visited Lithuania. We don't even know where exactly he died. I can't remember his face. Only this picture. When I was little, my mother told me a story about him trying to conquer a large city and dying during the attack. But I think she made that up. This morning she said that last night was a sign."

"Of what?"

"That he keeps watch over us, and that everything will be fine."

I handed back the picture and promised not to tell anyone

about it. That same night, though, when my mother came to my room and wouldn't stop asking me about the Madelungs, I broke that promise. Friedrich had seen his father's ghost, I told her; my cheeks were glowing with excitement. My mother listened greedily. She sat close to me, stroking my hair and listening intently. When I had told her everything I knew, her fingers trembled, and as though she was trying to gain control of her feelings, she bit her hand until she was bleeding. "A gift," she said with a hoarse voice. "What a gift."

"She thinks it's a good sign."

"My mother stared at me with wide-open eyes. "Certainly. Yes, there's no question."

That night the wind turned and rattled our windows, and when I looked outside the next morning, everything was buried under a fresh blanket of snow. Our truck refused to start, and when my father finally managed to bring the engine to life, the snow fell so heavily that we had to turn around after only a kilometer or two and head back home. As if the winter wanted to make up for lost time, it snowed without interruption for four days. The blossoms on the hedges froze and broke, the tree branches burst, and finally the canals froze over and Hemmer-smoor ground to a halt.

That first morning Jens Jensen, the old peat cutter, was lying drunk in a ditch, only his face and chest protruding from the snow. The children, who found him half-naked and half-frozen, threw snowballs at the slowly awakening man. "Where are my pants?" he asked in a rusty voice. "What have you done with them?"

My mother sighed in relief—for her the snow was a godsend. My father had to stay home and couldn't see Inge Madelung anymore. And every morning she waited for the mailman, stood by the window, and couldn't quiet her hands. When, on the third day, he finally fought his way through the snowdrifts and told her that he'd been to the manor house and delivered a thick envelope from the authorities to the widow, she hugged him. "Has to be her pension," he said and winked at her. "They must have declared her husband dead." After he left us, my mother stood by the window and cried for a long time.

That winter I understood very little of what was going on around me. I understood my mother's sorrow and the fears and suspicions she harbored, but the visits from the neighbors' wives and the mailman's curious behavior I couldn't explain. Something monstrous was happening under our roof, but I couldn't make the various parts fit. Instead I wished I could have gone with Anke to Groß Ostensen. I wished we could have owned a larger house, one that looked more like the Hoffmanns'. I wished I could have seen the ghost of Friedrich's father with my own eyes.

When, two days before Epiphany, the roads were accessible once again, I drove with my father to the manor house one final time. To my surprise Inge didn't greet us, and when I knocked on the Madelungs' door, everything stayed quiet. Inge had not waited for the snow to melt. The old owner came to deliver the news. "She left us," he said. Inge had packed the same suitcase with which she had arrived in Hemmersmoor. She had wrapped Friedrich in his thick coat and left for Hamburg. "I promised her a better room, but she didn't want to listen. God knows what got into her."

When I told my mother, she hugged me fiercely, kissed my cheeks and forehead, and made my father's favorite dish—pork roast with salt potatoes, carrots, and peas. Her steps were as light as a ballerina's. And even if my father remained silent during the following days, slowly peace was restored in our house.

Only in February did the weather break, and at the beginning of March the peat cutters were once again out on the canals. My mother had feared that Inge might return, but with every new day she gained more confidence. And even my dad, who for weeks had rarely said a word at the dinner table, smiled again when I showed him my homework or what I had painted in class. Inge Madelung had found a better home. She was able to start a new life. The women in our village didn't miss her.

It was a mild afternoon in April when we learned that Inge had never arrived in Hamburg. Peat cutters found her on their trek across the moor. The widow must have lost her way during the snowstorm, they said. Inge and Friedrich had died two kilometers from the road to Groß Ostensen. Klaus Schürholz found a letter from the Groß Ostensen authorities in Inge's pocket. It was exactly as the mailman had said. The good news about receiving her pension, the *Gendarm* reported, had caused the widow's death.

"A tragedy," the women in Meier's bakery called it when my mother and I went shopping after school had let out. "She wouldn't have had to pinch every penny anymore," Mrs. Meier said. "How foolish to walk across the moor during all that snow. A shame," Mrs. Schürholz cried. "That old von Kamphoff should have driven her to Groß Ostensen, the old cheapskate." My mother didn't know what to say to all this and completely forgot what it was she had come to buy. She stammered, stuttered, looked stunned at Mrs. Meier, and swayed lightly until her friend said, "Pull yourself together."

It was an accident. A foolish mistake. That's what everyone in the village said. And yet, wasn't it peculiar that my mother, who had wished nothing more than to see Inge Madelung driven from the manor, took the news of her death so badly? Wasn't it strange that she walked home from the bakery with her face all pale and drawn and that she buried her head in her hands all afternoon and cried bitterly?

Christian

Our father was a slight man, working as a foreman for the small dairy in Hemmersmoor.

In his youth, he had dreamt of leaving his village for Australia or Canada. He'd bought illustrated books about those countries and studied the photographs with his characteristic seriousness, as though it took a straight face and an inquiring mind to leaf through their pages. He would never have relaxed that face to smile or joke about the strange uniforms the police were wearing in the pictures, not for anything in the world. It might have shattered him to hear his own laughter in Canada's wild mountains.

Before getting married, he'd been driving a motorcycle, and he and my mother had been going to dances in the surrounding villages. A photo of them sat on a chest of drawers in the living room, and next to it was one in which my father stood in a leather jacket next to his milk-delivery van. Mr. Meier, the baker, had his right hand on my father's shoulder, and behind them several men who looked like soldiers were unloading bread and milk. The picture was taken during the war, but my dad and the baker had stayed in Hemmersmoor. They smiled at the camera.

My father was well liked in the village and among my friends. He was charming, friendly, and the year I turned eleven and my sister's belly swelled up was a good one for him.

By November, Nicole's belly stuck out like a watermelon, and she wasn't allowed to leave the house. "Who was it?" I asked her, like my mother had countless times before. Yet I didn't shower her face with punches, I didn't bang her head against the bedpost. My sister Ingrid had died four years ago in the fall. "And now we're losing this one too," my mother lamented.

I stroked Nicole's belly, which I could barely stand to look at but had to touch nonetheless. I couldn't keep my fingers off it. What was inside knocked against my hand, and my sister's face grew terrified; another person possessed her like a demon. She was fifteen.

"Who was it?" I wanted to know. She had to have done it—I knew how people were made. I had watched Alex's sister do it with an apprentice from Brümmer's factory. It was an ugly business, brutal, and yet Alex and I had used every opportunity we'd gotten to watch through his floorboards how the young guy shook and groaned and how Anna's flesh quivered like pudding.

My sister smiled at my questions and kept silent. My mother announced to Hemmersmoor that Nicole was sick, and kept a close eye on me. "If you don't watch your mouth," she promised, "you will forever regret it." Since my sister Ingrid's death, she had nothing but harsh words for me. My toes bled whenever she trimmed my nails, and one day in the fall she had poured boiling water onto my lap and later said the saucepan had slipped out of her grip. Whenever she caught me in Nicole's room, she cursed at me and called my sister a whore.

My dad was more forgiving and devoted himself to my sister's care. They'd always been close; he'd taken naps with her in the afternoon until she was eight, and he called her *Mieze*. Now he brought her dinner when she felt too weak to come down from her room.

I could have put it together myself if I had known how to connect my thoughts, moods, and observations. Yet it was Alex who, one day after school, asked, "What are you going to do with the bastard?"

I stared at him; I hadn't told him about the baby. "Nicole is sick," I said dutifully.

Alex's bushy eyebrows met above his nose—he stared that hard at me. He was one class ahead of me in school and knew everything a year in advance. "My mom says she knows that kind of sickness. She also says it's strange that your parents haven't tried to pin it on someone. She says that if she were your mom, she'd be all over town defending her daughter's honor."

"Nicole won't tell me who it was," I said.

"Mom says there's no one your folks can blame. It's either God's baby, or the devil's, and the former hasn't happened in two thousand years, so it's the devil's."

"The devil's?" I asked.

"Your dad's," Alex said. "I think that's what she means."

The suggestion was so utterly impossible that I immediately knew it was true. That night at dinner, all the glances, silences, and quiet words suddenly made sense to me, as if I had learned a new language and for the first time was able to follow the conversation.

I realized that my mother administered her beatings, not to find out the truth, but solely to punish, and that my dad's smiles were not fueled by forgiveness but expectations. He was looking forward to seeing his child.

I sneaked into my sister's room after my parents had gone to bed. I pushed up her nightshirt and put my ear to her belly. My father was in there, small and unborn.

"What is going to happen to him?" I asked.

Nicole shook her head. She was beautiful in a quiet way. You wouldn't have noticed her in a crowd, and yet once you'd spied her, you realized she could beat out any girl in Hemmersmoor. I was convinced we had to act quickly. The baby was due in March, and who knew what Mom and Dad had planned? There was only one way to make sure neither Nicole nor her child would be harmed.

I did not tell Nicole of my plans; I did not want to burden her. No, I had to do it all by myself. Yet what could I possibly do without arousing suspicion? I tried to remember spells I'd heard mentioned in the village. I asked my friends to recount what they knew about ghouls, witches, and wizards. Time passed uneasily, and still I hadn't come up with a solution. Soon it would be Christmas.

On the first day of Advent, I ran over to Frick's Inn to visit Alex. His mother had died the year before, and he helped in the pub in the afternoons and on weekends. His brother had long since left the village and sailed to New York. Nobody knew if and when he would return, and Hilde, his young wife, had moved into the apartment above the inn. "I had to move back to my old room," Alex complained.

While I was waiting for my friend, I overheard a conversation at the bar. A candle had been lit in the pine wreath hanging from the ceiling. Jens Jensen, who'd come right after church as always, sat at the bar with a fresh glass of beer in front of him.

"You've got to be careful that night. It's the darnedest thing," said the old man, while drinking his beer and scratching his gray stubble. "If you drink wine that night, you'll be dead by Epiphany."

"What night would that be?" I asked. Alex was getting gloves and a hat from upstairs, and I couldn't let this chance go by.

"Who wants to know?" Jens Jensen turned away from the farmer's wife he'd been talking to, a woman with broken veins webbing her face. Her husband slept peacefully by the fireplace.

"It's me, Christian."

"The Bobinski boy," he said, looking me over. "Christmas Eve, of course."

"What happens on Christmas Eve?" I said.

Jens Jensen took a long drink from his beer, foam gathering on his lip. "Why, when you get up during the night before Christmas," he said with importance, "you'll notice an enormous thirst."

"You always have an enormous thirst," the farmer's wife said and laughed boomingly at her own joke.

"Right you are," Jensen said, and slapped her knee affectionately. "Go to hell, sweetheart." Then he turned once more to me. "On Christmas Eve you can drink nothing but water."

Alex arrived with his hat and gloves and started pulling me away, but I shook him off.

"So what if you don't drink water?" I said.

"If you drink wine that night," the old peat cutter said, lowering his voice for effect, "you won't stop drinking. You'll drink yourself to death before the star singers are home." He grinned, exposing more gaps than teeth. "When I was your age—"

"You were born old," the farmer's wife boomed, slapping her hand on the counter.

"When I was your age," Jensen said again, "we knew these things." He extended a hand, maybe to touch my face, but I pulled back. He laughed. "We all knew these things, and they're still true, but no one remembers." He looked at me with eyes that didn't even seem to recognize me anymore. "We've forgotten the traps."

"Let's go," Alex said impatiently, and this time I followed him outside.

The weeks before Christmas were as serene and light filled as they had ever been, but that year I hardly noticed the smell of gingerbread cookies, of cinnamon, vanilla, and oranges. The people of Hemmersmoor seemed to live in a story of good cheer and happy preparations, a story of warmth and expectations I couldn't squeeze into. I still went to school, still helped my dad cut a tree near the ruins of the Black Mill, still helped Mom with baking cookies, but I didn't understand what I was doing. It didn't register. Because Advent was just as it always had been, it didn't make any sense to me anymore.

Mom's attacks on Nicole receded like a tide. I tended to my sister and her belly every evening, and should Nicole fall asleep before I had left, I would talk to the baby. I let my hand rest above the navel and murmured words to the infant, who was growing bigger, making a room for itself inside Nicole. "You're safe," I'd say. "Don't worry. I'll make it right once you get out."

I made a point of being obedient to my parents, especially my dad. When we cut down the pine tree, I let him tell me the story of the Black Miller again, as though I'd never heard it before. The mill had been empty for centuries but still withstood wind and rain and snow; the miller's ghost kept everything in working order and was still out for revenge. Halfway through the tale of how Swedish soldiers had raped the miller's daughters, my father stopped to look at me sideways, from under his fur-lined hat.

"Have you any interest in girls yet?" he said.

I stared at him, clutching my axe. He was still taller and stronger than me, but in that moment my thoughts focused on how to split his skull in half. It was a possibility. I shook my head.

"Never too early," he chuckled. "It'll come soon. Just make sure to marry a girl that's not all used up. You can have fun with many, but those you can't marry."

I nodded.

"The best way to start is with an experienced woman," he said, cleaning off the lower branches of our tree. "A married woman." And then he told me how he'd been initiated as a fifteen-year-old boy by an older cousin in Groß Ostensen and how he was still thankful to that woman. "She made me a man," he said. I gritted my teeth.

On the ride home, he nudged me with his elbow. "I'm glad we had this talk. I want to be your good friend. If you have problems with a girl—I know a thing or two. Just ask."

On Christmas Eve my nerves were strung so tight that my head ached and I couldn't sit still. I endured the morning chores, chewed through the obligatory lunch of sausages and potato salad. In the afternoon I bundled up. Under the pretense of having something important to do in preparation for the *Bescherung*, the exchanging and unwrapping of gifts that evening after dinner, I hurried outside.

We hardly ever had snow on Christmas. In our village snow and ice would arrive a week or two later and stay until February. Now it was merely cold, and rain was falling softly. Yet the weather did nothing to soothe me. I was a prisoner in my body. I should have been able to rip it open and escape, but I was stuck in my flesh, stuck in my family, stuck in Hemmersmoor. Nothing fit.

I ran down to the Droste, where Sylvia, a girl some years older than me, was standing on the bank, throwing small stones and branches into the water.

"Hi," I said.

"Hi," she said without interest.

"Aren't you home?" I asked stupidly.

She laughed at the question, but nicely. "No, I'm not. I'm waiting," she said.

"For what?" I asked.

"For someone," she corrected me, blushing.

"For whom?" I asked.

"Don't be nosy."

"You could bless me," I said.

"Like a priest?"

"Yes."

"What for?"

"I don't know," I lied.

She stepped closer and put her hand on my hair. "I bless

you," she said, and before I could stop her, she had kissed my forehead. "Merry Christmas," she said.

I left her without saying good-bye, suddenly feeling ashamed. I ran as fast as I could until my shirt clung to my skin and the sweat turned icy. If I got sick, I wouldn't have to do a thing. Sickness was the only thing that came close to leaving one's body. I ran.

The scolding from my mother hardly registered with me, and I took her lamentations over my wet and muddy pants and boots in silence. I didn't complain about the hot bath, or about the beating I received at her hands, and how my ears started to ring because I didn't fend her off. I didn't complain about the stiff collar of my shirt or about my pants being too short and tight. I felt defeated by the task ahead of me.

After eating the goose my mother had been cooking since the afternoon and then washing the dishes, we opened our presents. My sister received wide shirts and loose-fitting dresses, as well as big bras and panties. She was very quiet while unwrapping them, shrinking from the enormous items. She feared the person who would wear them. She remained quiet while I unwrapped books and a toy train, stared at them with greed.

Around ten we blew out the few remaining lights on the tree and prepared to go to sleep. I'm not sure anyone did. My mother had to notice the empty space next to her, even though by now she'd grown accustomed to it.

Myself, I waited near the door of my sister's room until the silence I could feel coming through the wall and door, dense as the cooking smells that had come all day from my mother's kitchen, grew thin and cold. Moments later my father emerged, heading to the bathroom.

I sat on the stairs until he reemerged, and then kicked the banister.

"Who's there?" he asked.

I slunk down the stairs, waiting for him to follow me. Sure enough, by the time I sat next to the Christmas tree, holding the train in my hands, he had made his way down the stairs.

"Is that you, Christian?" he said, relieved. He was holding a slipper in his hand like a weapon, his left foot was naked.

"Yes," I said.

"Couldn't sleep, huh?" He asked softly. "Are the gifts the right ones?"

"Yes," I said. "I had to look again." After a pause, I added, "I'm thirsty."

"Me too," my father said. He put on his left slipper, and in the faint glow of the room seemed to smile. "Let's have a little midnight snack, shall we?"

From the fridge, he took sausages and milk, and I got the bread from the breadbox. "Is there some mulled wine left?" I asked.

The question made my dad chuckle. "You had a glass already."

"Please?"

Soon we reheated the wine. While I was careful only to raise my glass without drinking, my father emptied his while chewing on the leftover sausages. We ate like two starving beggars, as if we'd never before eaten goose and stuffing and potatoes and greens and pudding. We ate and he drank.

By one o'clock I lay in bed wide awake. I didn't feel guilt over what I had done, but my plan seemed too enormous to think through. Just like the sausages and bread and goose, my thoughts kept me awake all night, until gray light scurried over the floor like mice.

My father never made it to breakfast. He refused to eat, stayed in bed all day. Yet he drank. My mother had to go down to the cellar and carry bottles of wine upstairs. She was concerned, bewildered, yet after refusing at first and earning harsh words, she relented.

For the two days of Christmas, my father drank. He ate little, and what little he ate, he emptied into the toilet bowl shortly. On the twenty-seventh he went to work but was sent home early after fainting. The doctor came and prescribed medicine, and my father took the powders and tablets and drank. He drank and drank, and after he'd gone through the modest reserves of our cellar, he made my mother buy more. He drank until his sweat turned pink and the bedroom reeked like Frick's Inn. Still he didn't stop. He didn't seem to get drunk. He didn't grow loud. He drank only to sleep feverishly, wake up, and drink more.

On the last day of Christmas, January 6, he died. A shadow lifted from our house; his revenge, which I'd felt would destroy me should he recover, died with him. He was buried in our cemetery, and half of Hemmersmoor came out to pay him their last respects.

Despite the dark, stuffy clothes I was wearing, I felt unburdened. I watched the burial with a sense of success, and I slept soundly that night.

I still visited my sister, who'd not been allowed to attend the funeral, and who looked scared and miserable. I should have kept quiet, but the ease with which I had accomplished our liberation went to my head. One day in late February, a day before

I turned twelve, my sister was crying in fear of her giant belly, and I told her what I had risked for her sake. She didn't have to be afraid anymore, I said. He was gone, and I would take care of her once I was old enough to earn money.

"I saved you," I told Nicole, and explained how I had done it.

She slapped me, took the teapot from her nightstand, and broke it on my head. She beat me with her fists and wouldn't have stopped had the child not started to move inside her.

After that night I was only reluctantly tolerated in our house, and soon my back was scarred, my arms burned, my body full of bruises. Whenever someone commented on my cuts and scabs, I shrugged and said, "A real boy needs scars."

My mother and sister raised the child, a boy, together. A refugee from that other Germany had taken advantage of my sister, they said when they wheeled the baby through the village. They told me to keep my dirty mouth shut. And so I repeated what they had taught me: a kid from the East had done it.

Martin

After the New Year, the canals crisscrossing the peat bog froze, and as soon as school was out we chased each other across the ice. I had inherited my father's red hair and hid it underneath black woolen hats, which I pulled down over my forehead. But I couldn't do anything about the freckles, which spread on my face even in the dead of winter. I was thirteen and felt alternately ugly and invisible.

As soon as the ice was thick enough, lovers chose the night to glide to far and hidden corners of the bog, and our parents still talked about the winter when Julian Fitschen and Anna Jensen melted through the ice because they had lost control of their feelings. The lovers were lifted from the water frozen solid, carried into the village like a pagan statue, and left to stand in back of the Fitschens' farm until spring.

Sometimes my friends Alex, Christian, Holger, Bernhard, and I would go to where the Droste River slowed and widened into a lake, and ice fish. We'd pick holes in the ice and cast our lines. Yet we ran out of patience soon and rarely caught a fish.

On one of these trips, Broder, the Hoffmanns' youngest son, accompanied us, carrying an axe as tall as his lithe body. It had been years since I had played with his sister, Anke, and Linde Janeke and braided their hair. We had often watched the girls with a mixture of repulsion and amusement, had pulled at their braids and pushed and teased them after school. Now, however, we looked at them with new interest. Last year Alex had fallen mortally in love with Anke and had tried to get her to unbutton her blouse, and she had declined. He'd tried the whole fall and had enlisted Broder as the messenger for his lovelorn letters. Alex had since found a new object for his pursuits, but Broder still clung to him, no matter how hard Alex tried to get rid of the boy.

"I'll bring you luck," Broder crowed happily. He'd been a star singer, caroling in a cardboard crown painted gold, his voice bright and high.

We laughed. Our own voices were a mess; we preferred silence. We were going to high school in Groß Ostensen, ten kilometers to the south. We were old enough to wish ourselves beyond Hemmersmoor, yet we were too young to buy mopeds and drive to Groß Ostensen's movie theater and ice cream parlor. When the townspeople talked about us, the word "incest" cropped up frequently. We looked at their world and their girls, and they didn't look back.

When we reached the Droste River, we put on our skates and took off toward the middle, where the ice responded with shrieks and pangs to our weight. It was around three o'clock in the afternoon, and groups of kids slid or skated over the lake. The sun had not bothered to come out, and the light was already fading. Snow fell, tickling our faces.

"What happens if the ice breaks?" Broder asked.

"We'll drown," I said.

"Why, Martin?" he asked. "I can swim."

"Your skates," I said. "They're too heavy. Your clothes will pull you down."

Alex took out a pack of cigarettes and offered them around. His father gave him money for the work he did around the inn; the rest of us couldn't afford to smoke. We skated lazily, smoked, on the lookout for a good spot to fish. The snow rendered the small kids near the banks invisible and turned us invisible to them. We could have been on a vast ocean, lost in the middle of the Baltic Sea. It was a good feeling.

"Here. That's our spot," Alex said.

"Here. That's the spot," Broder echoed. We picked and hammered away.

"Look how thick it is," Broder said.

"Look how thick it is," Alex mocked him, but the boy laughed it off.

In time we cast our lines, sat on our haunches, smoking. We enjoyed the solitude until we were shivering. You're supposed to have a hut or a fire, and we didn't have either. Our bones rattled, our teeth chattered. Nobody caught a thing.

"So where's the luck you promised?" Alex said.

"Just a little longer," Broder replied. "You'll see." He closed his eyes so tightly that his small face was all wrinkles. "I can feel it."

"You didn't bring me any luck with your sister," Alex said.

"She didn't like you," Broder said brightly. We all laughed; it was the truth. Even quiet Christian laughed. He was a pale boy, his hair and eyebrows so light he looked naked. He had lost his father two years before, and when he changed his sports clothes at school, we could see scrapes and bruises on his arms and back. But he never complained.

"No girl likes you," Bernhard said. "Your mind's too dirty." Bernhard still had no beard but was the tallest and heaviest of us all. His face was as pretty as a girl's.

"Shut up," Alex said. "Anke hurt me."

Holger grunted. He was heavyset and had short dark hair and a red face with even redder cheeks. His feet were already larger than those of most grown men. "Anke won't go for you."

"Why not?" Alex asked. His brown mustache was frozen, his small eyes framed by icy white lashes. "If my brother doesn't return, I'll inherit the inn and the land and will be richer than the Hoffmanns."

Alex's brother was a sailor, and after leaving for New York one day, he had never returned to his wife. Postcards from around the world arrived irregularly in our village.

"Why shouldn't he come back?" I asked.

"Maybe he's contracted leprosy or maybe he'll drown. Who knows? If it were up to me, the ship's kobold could carry him off."

"But if he returns?"

"I'll deal with him then. The inn is mine, and if Anke won't have me, I'll buy her family's farm and have her brothers cut my peat." He focused on Broder. "Right?"

"Right," Broder said. "I'll cut peat."

"She won't be able to find a better man," Alex said, more to himself.

I nodded. I wasn't as strong as Holger or as pretty as Bernhard. Nor was my family as well-heeled as Alex's, which owned Frick's Inn. Yet I had kissed Linde Janeke before Christmas break and considered myself ahead of the others. Linde wasn't as beautiful as Anke, but she had been seen with a boy from Groß Ostensen who rode a moped and was seventeen. That counted for something.

It was around the time we lost any feeling in our feet that Alex dropped his hatchet in the water.

"What'd you do that for?" Holger said.

"You're stupid," Bernhard chimed in. "That hatchet is gone."

"Maybe." Alex pulled out a ten-mark bill. "Maybe someone is willing to dive after the hatchet for ten."

We laughed at his offer. Christian tapped his finger to his forehead and rolled his eyes.

"Okay," Alex said, pulling out another bill. "Twenty. I'll give you twenty if you can get the hatchet."

"Keep your money," I said, stretching my legs. I was ready to head home.

"I could," Broder said. His eyes were large; the things he could buy for twenty marks! You could see his mind at work, his head filling with possibilities. "But I won't. I'm not stupid."

We laughed. "Good call," Bernhard said. "No one's that stupid."

"But I'll do it for fifty."

We shook our heads, still grinning, gathering our lines and tools.

"I'll do it," Broder repeated, more loudly. He took off his coat. "For fifty."

"Man," Bernhard said, "put your coat back on. You'll freeze to death like that without having to dive."

"Fifty," Broder crowed.

"Wait," Christian said and fished in his pockets. "I have a five, a ten, and three ones." He lay the bills and coins on the ground, then grabbed Alex's two tens and put them on top.

Bernhard whistled. "Guys, that's dumb. Look, even if he doesn't die from the cold, he's not going to find that damn hatchet, and he's not going to find this shitty hole again when he comes up for air."

"I can do it." Broder took off his skates and shoes.

Holger came up with another eight marks, and I provided the rest. Alex put Broder's shoe on top of the pile and looked at the kid. "Fifty," he said.

"Wait!" Bernhard raised his right hand like a teacher, begging for silence. "How are we going to dry him off? If he comes back up."

"Shut up," Alex growled. "My grandpa used to take baths in the Droste all winter long, and he's still around." He turned to Broder. "Okay, we've got fifty marks."

The boy stripped to his underwear, then stood by the rim of the ice. Around us the air was filled with snow and darker than the ground, and it was very quiet, except for Broder sucking in the air and blowing his nose. The snow must have been a shower of a thousand needles.

"I can do it," he said and looked once more at the pile of money. Then he jumped, feet first, pinching his nose. The water took him.

We soon found ourselves crouching at the hole, our hearts louder than the protesting ice. We were feverish, we suddenly knew that we'd have to explain later, and that no one would forgive us for what we'd done, and we knew in our hearts that Broder would never come up, had never stood a chance. And yet. And yet as long as we could hold our breaths with him, he might pull it off. He might. The fifty marks said so.

The Droste River was only three to four meters deep where

we stood, and we had often touched the bottom on lazy summer days, but this was January; this was an eight-year-old boy. And yet.

We expected to hear knocking, and searched the ice. Was Broder caught under the thick sheet? Had Bernhard been right? Was it impossible to find the opening?

"He's dead," Bernhard finally said, his mouth twitching.

"He's dead," I said, having counted slowly to sixty. My four marks lay in the snow. What would I have given to never have offered them?

Bernhard didn't stop crying when Broder's head appeared in front of us. He cried louder, and we all shouted in rough voices and lifted the boy out of the water. He was red as if we'd boiled him. In his right hand he held the hatchet. "It was so dark," Broder stammered. "So dark. I couldn't see a thing down there, and when I came up, I didn't know where I was. A moment longer and I would have swallowed water." He went on like this, while we tried to wipe him dry with his shirt. "So dark I had to feel for the hatchet on the ground. And there were slimy things, and once I felt that something was grabbing my leg and pulling me farther down. It pulled and pulled and wouldn't let go." His whole body twitched and shivered, and words poured from him, in awe of being with us again, in awe of what he had just done and how he had shown us.

Holger took off his brown scarf and helped dry the boy, rubbing his face and hair.

"Wait," Alex said. He took the wet hatchet and threw it back down in our fishing hole. "You did it once," he said. "Fifty marks. It's a lot of money for a bit of cold. Come on, Broder, it's easy. Just once more."

The boy turned to Alex and grinned, not sure whether or not it was a joke. I stared at Alex, stared at Broder. We held wet scarves and shirts in our hands and stared from one to the other. There didn't seem to be a single sound left in this world.

Then Broder jumped.

We threw his shoes and clothes after him that night, along with the fifty marks. We made a solemn pact to keep quiet forever.

Bernhard didn't keep his word though, and the Hoffmanns went to the police and refused to take the money Alex's father offered them. All five of us were guilty, but the Hoffmanns went easy on the rest of us. They wanted Alex. It had been his idea. It had been his axe.

After dark Mr. Frick came to see my father, the *Gendarm*, and I could hear them talking heatedly. They kept the door to the living room closed for long hours. My dad wanted to help him, but in the end he had no say in the matter. The Hoffmanns insisted on their rights. His hands were tied; he had to think of his own son. At the end of March, Alex was sent away for three years and the rest of us wished we could have left Hemmer-smoor too.

Linde

Three generations of the family had lived in the manor house by the time I was thirteen, but the old master no longer managed the place and had handed the reins over to his son. Bruno von Kamphoff was in his forties and looked more like his mother. He had nothing of his father's harshness of features. His eyes were big, brown, and melancholy, his fingers and limbs pale and long. He played the piano as frequently as the old mistress. He was not well liked in the village because he was "weak." He was "effeminate." Be that as it may, he knew how to handle his vast staff comprising a cook, maids, several butlers, a chauffeur, and farmhands working the land. Finally, of course, they had my father, who came every day in his cranky old truck with only one wheel in front, a once innovative design that already in my early childhood had been an object of much ridicule. Bruno never paid my dad more than the old von Kamphoff had.

His wife had once been a famous singer in Hamburg, and the apothecary's wife swore that she'd been a harlot in some St. Pauli revue before becoming mistress of the Big House. Karin von Kamphoff wasn't beautiful but striking. Her features were clear-cut; she had a large nose, a large mouth, large blue eyes, and a high forehead. Her body was padded "in all the right places," as the men of Hemmersmoor observed, and on Christmas Eve she still sang to guests while her husband accompanied her on the piano. "These days," the apothecary's wife said, "she doesn't have to undress to get what she wants."

Rumors abounded, as they did with every family who lived somewhat removed from our eyes. The basement was filled with war loot, one said; the basement was used for black masses, went another. Bastard children were popular, as was the black woman Johann von Kamphoff supposedly captured during the war and held hostage in his basement. The most enduring legend, however, was that of the real heir. The real heir, the customers in Frick's Inn contended, was as real as the sun and stars, and many proclaimed to have seen him until about forty years ago, when he'd vanished in infancy. He'd been Johann's younger brother, and because of a violent fight between Johann and his father had been made the heir of the manor. Yet he hadn't been spotted since before the wars, and many a night it was speculated that Johann had everything to do with his disappearance. If he should ever return, Bruno would lose everything.

Bruno von Kamphoff's children, Rutger and Sophie, were twenty and seventeen the summer I accompanied my father to the Big House. Their parents' clashing physical attributes had endowed them with great beauty, and the villagers admired and despised them for it. Of course we hardly saw them in Hemmersmoor, since the von Kamphoffs had never attended our school. They were educated by private teachers from Hamburg and Bremen who lived in one wing of the Big House or another.

At my age habit and new discoveries were at war within me. I loved my father, loved following him around and listening to instructions on how and when to cut rosebushes, but I also wanted to know who my friend Anke was making out with, what the best ways were to bewitch a boy's heart, and how to smoke without coughing.

I often visited Ilse Westerholt, the oldest daughter of our neighbors, and borrowed barrettes or dresses from her. I didn't have any siblings—"How should we feed them?" my mother said—and Ilse braided my hair endlessly, washed and scrubbed my face until it hurt, and showed me how to pluck my eyebrows. I hoped to earn adoring looks or a whistle from the groups of older boys who hung around outside Frick's Inn on their mopeds.

It was six years after Friedrich and his mother had died, and the last summer I went out to the von Kamphoffs. Many days I didn't even get up at five to have coffee with dad and take my seat next to him in the truck. When I did go, I felt awkward standing next to my father and lending him a hand. I seemed too big, too energetic, too grown, and too pretty to still walk by his side.

One morning, after the old von Kamphoff had walked over from the Big House to pay us a visit, I used the men's conversation to steal away. The night before, Johann Jensen had asked me to go out with him on Saturday, and I had promised him an answer by tonight. This was a difficult decision. Johann was handsome, nineteen, had a motorcycle and a job at Brümmer's factory. But if I went with him, I'd forego possible dates with Torsten Pott, who topped my list and was currently unattached. He was a good friend of Johann's, and once I'd settled for Johann, Torsten might be beyond my reach. Then there was Martin, the *Gendarm*'s son, who'd asked me for a barrette I'd worn when we'd run into each other the previous week. Was he serious about me? He was only sixteen and owned no moped, only an old bicycle. Last winter he'd been with the other boys the day Broder Hoffmann drowned. But only Alex Frick had been found guilty and sent to a correctional facility. Since that accident, Martin acted different, seemed older, more mature than even Torsten. Anke said she liked Martin best but that none of my admirers had a future and that her mother had admonished her that we should save ourselves for better men. I was in a quandary.

My favorite part of the vast grounds around the Big House was the maze. It had been designed more than a hundred years ago, and its hedges were almost twice as tall as me. Once you entered it, even the brightest day darkened, and it gave me the feeling that as long as I wandered inside it, I did not belong to the petty world of beat-up trucks, school, and chores, nor would anybody be able to reach me with his voice.

Over the years I had gained knowledge of the maze's layout, but since my visits to the Big House had been sporadic lately and my thoughts were occupied with boys, hairdos, and nail polish, I soon found myself lost. Once you lost your bearings in the maze, it proved next to impossible to regain them, and since the sun had yet to find her way out of the clouds, I had no point of orientation. This did not concern me, however. Although the maze was vast, covering more than a hectare of land and keeping many of my father's helpers busy every other week in the summer, I had time enough on my hands to find my way out. The day had only just begun. In fact, I greeted my confusion, which, should my father have reason to ask, would provide me with a welcome excuse.

During my many visits to the maze, I had learned that the von Kamphoffs did not share my love for its shady paths. They had forbidden the children to enter the maze for fear they should harm themselves, and never had I encountered the master or mistress near it. Yet my dad, even though I knew he had often tried to steer the conversation toward its possible demise, had not been allowed to reduce the size or do away with the maze.

Imagine my bewilderment when I suddenly spied another figure ahead of me, turning quickly and vanishing from sight. I shrieked. I was certain that none of my father's helpers was working on the hedges that day, nor did I believe for a second that the master or his wife had entered the maze. Who, then, was the intruder?

I waited with a galloping heart for several minutes, then decided that whoever it had been was far enough away for me to seek my way out of the maze. I walked along one wall and turned left, since I'd learned from my father to make only left turns if I should ever lose my way. No sooner had I rounded the first corner, than I bumped into the trespasser.

"You found me," he shrieked in delight, and I shrieked back, and so we shrieked for many seconds until I had exhausted myself and was quite convinced that the stranger posed no imminent danger to me.

He was a curious man. His age was hard to guess—it had to be somewhere past thirty and not over sixty-five, but a better estimate was beyond me. He had lines and wrinkles, yet nevertheless his skin seemed very fresh and smooth. He was no taller than me and stood stooped and flailed his arms and jumped about like someone half my age.

"Shall we do it again?" he asked and was gone as soon as he'd proposed it.

"Wait," I shouted, but received no answer. Who was this man? He wasn't from Hemmersmoor. I'd never seen him in the village, and he wasn't dressed like a villager. He wasn't dressed like anyone I'd ever seen. He wore a white shirt large enough to reach his thighs and white pants that were soiled at the knees, as though he'd fallen often or crawled about. He wore a slipper on his left foot and the right was bare. His thin hair was short and cut in the style popular in our village: a pot had been put over his head and all the hair sticking out sheared off.

After he was gone from my sight, I hesitated to continue, but my curiosity won out over my apprehension, and soon I was following the turns of the maze, spying around corners. At an intersection I was debating whether to take a left or right, when my eyes went blind.

"You're not so good, are you?" the stranger said into my ear. "I could die of an empty tummy before you found me."

I jerked my head free and stared directly into his brown eyes. "You're not allowed to move," I protested. "You have to stay in one place."

"Says who?"

"That's the rule."

"It is?" he asked, making a sad face. "I had no idea."

"How else could I find you?"

"You didn't."

"Because you kept moving."

"Is that so?" He seemed to really think about it. "All right," he finally concluded. "It's your turn."

I did as he said, following the stupid hide-and-seek routine without further questions. Had I paused, I would have tried to scale a hedge and run away, but the stranger's urgent voice, which sounded like dishes clattering in the sink, left me no time for such thoughts. I hid.

Within two seconds, he stood next to me.

"You followed me," I complained.

"So?" he asked.

"That's against the rules."

"Says who?"

"The rules," I said, suddenly growing annoyed. "What are you doing here anyway? Do you live in the Big House?"

"Not now," the stranger said. "I live here."

"Who are you?" I said. I had never much spoken to any of the von Kamphoffs, and when I'd done so, never without a curtsy. Yet this man was different, I understood, and politeness not required.

"I am a professor," he said.

"Of what?" I asked. I knew little of professors, had never set foot in a university, and knew no one who had. Still I knew these creatures had specialties.

"Of what?" he echoed. "Of this maze, of course. Of mathematics, religion, and world history."

"How can you be a professor of this maze?" I asked.

"I'm also a king and chop off many heads. If there's a man or woman who insults me, I chop off their head." He made a cutting motion with his hand, as if slicing an onion.

His reply made me afraid again. I realized that this old man might be a lunatic, and that he had probably escaped from the asylum near Groß Ostensen. "I should go," I said.

He bowed. "Don't say a word. Or else." He made the chopping motion.

Yet I had been walking for only a few minutes before I was back where I had left him.

"Hello?" he said.

"I need to get out," I said.

He shrugged his shoulders. Oddly, he seemed to have forgotten that we'd just met, because he didn't rise from the grass or look a second time at me.

"Can you help me?" I asked.

"Do you need a horse?" he asked.

I ran off again, and this time I made it out of the maze. My breath was rattling, my heart pounding in my ears. Every second longer that I had spent in the maze had aggravated me, and I felt like crying for help. Yet as soon as I stepped onto the lawn, the manor house only a few hundred yards to my left, I felt only the deepest disappointment. The danger was over; the day had lost its luster.

I longed to tell my father about my strange adventure but honored the promise I had given. The man had seemed harmless enough that I did not feel it necessary to betray his whereabouts. However, at night in my room—I had told Johann, my only suitor, no that evening in front of Frick's and was already regretting it—my thoughts wandered off to the Big House and into the maze. Was the stranger asleep among the hedges or awake like me, frightened by the night's dampness and countless small noises? Was he hungry? Then my mind drifted and for the first time I remembered the legends of the real heir and asked myself if I'd just met him. If the legend turned out to be true, how would the von Kamphoff family react to my discovery? What would Bruno say? Would he have to relinquish the manor? Would he beg me to keep what I knew a secret? Before my thoughts turned to dreams, this became more than just a possibility. The stranger was my key to the Big House.

In the morning I rose before my father, who smiled with satisfaction when he came into the kitchen and found the coffee ready. "Found your appetite again?" he said.

I nodded. Before leaving the house, I packed extra bread, a glass jar of jam, and several slices of ham and filled a bottle with water. I was eager to see the man again, against my better judgment.

On arrival my father was told by the steward that certain parts of the grounds were off-limits because "county inspectors were measuring the manor for tax purposes." Dad nodded, but after the steward left, he spit and said, "Humbug." Still, he had me do chores all morning and kept me at his side. It wasn't until I pretended to feel light-headed—a condition my father accepted as belonging to the world of female mysteries—that I could venture off with exact instructions where not to go.

The maze was forbidden, but I entered it nevertheless—too strong was my curiosity. Since I didn't want to draw the von Kamphoffs' attention, I had to look for the stranger without a sound. Shouting was not an option. Instead I walked and walked, careful not to run into any of the tax inspectors. I had already given up hope of ever finding the professor when I came to an enormous hole. Loose earth was lying in heaps beyond the hole and blocked the path entirely.

At the bottom of the hole sat the professor. His shirt was no longer white, his hands looked as dirty as my father's, and his fingers were full of dried blood. Blood and dirt covered his cheeks and forehead and pants. He sat perfectly erect on the ground, humming to himself.

"Hello," I said.

I received no reply.

"Hey there, Professor," I called.

He finally looked up, without recognizing me it seemed.

"Did you dig this hole?" I asked and climbed over a small mound of dirt, ready to join him in the pit.

"Be careful," he called. "Step gently."

"Of course," I replied, and, carrying the food for him in one hand and lifting my other for balance, I descended.

"Oh no," he cried when I landed, covering his ears with his trembling hands.

"What is it?" I asked, but had to ask again after he was done playing deaf.

"Didn't I ask you to be gentle?" he reprimanded me. "Your thoughtlessness might have caused us great harm."

"How so?" I asked, suppressing a laugh. He looked droll in his dirty clothes, much like a kid after an especially wild afternoon in the mud.

"One false step and we might break through the crust of the earth and fall out on the other side and into the skies and be lost."

I believed he was playing a prank on me, but when he moved closer toward me and took good care to be as careful as a thief at night, I understood that he was serious.

"I dug this hole to reach the other side, where dark people walk on their heads, but I'm afraid I might not be able to hold on to the earth once I get there. Maybe you could."

"I brought you food," I said, not knowing how to respond to the rubbish he'd told me.

"I'm not fond of the night," he said, making an important face. "The stars are cold and behind them angels are hiding and trying to suck in your breath to warm themselves." He unwrapped the bread and ham and said, "It's quite coarse," but ate nevertheless. He didn't wash his bloodied hands and chewed quite noisily.

"How will I pay you?" he asked when he had finished the last crumb and was scooping jam from the glass with two fingers.

"I don't need any pay," I said. "But answer me. Are you the real heir? The one everyone is talking about?"

"The real heir," he said. "Of what?"

"Of the Big House."

"Of course it's mine," he said. "All this is mine." He flailed his arms, which I took as a sign that he meant the whole manor.

"Then where have you been all these years? Why aren't you the master of it all?"

He looked at me with large eyes, seemingly uncomprehending. "It's mine," he repeated, "it's all mine, and I will make you my mistress." From the depths of his shirt he produced a leather bag, and from it he pulled a large golden key. "This gives you reign over my manor once I'm gone. It's my will, and you will be richer than the caliph of Baghdad."

I took the key and put it in my pocket. "How come I've never seen you before? Not once. All my life I've visited this place, but you weren't here."

"I've never seen you myself. And I've been here all my life." He laughed at his own remark, pleased with himself.

I waited for him to continue, but he fell silent, sitting in his hole, afraid to get up lest he might fall through the earth.

At last I left him, scrambled up and promised to bring him more food the next day. He responded by putting one jam-smeared finger to his mouth.

That evening my father was in a glum mood. As our truck bounced and coughed its way home, dad cursed Bruno von Kamphoff and his greed, he cursed the steward for interfering with his work, mother for always wanting more than he could provide, and he berated himself for being a lowly gardener and a poor husband. "I always thought I'd be blessed with all the good things," he said. "When I was a boy, I dreamed of adventures in the Far East and the Wild West. I'd travel the world like men do in novels. It was just a matter of growing up. And what happened? I became a gardener."

I knew this mood of his well. Maybe he had drunk from a flask he carried with him, or else my mother might have given him a hard time the night before. I shouldn't have paid attention to this mood, which came and went like bad weather. I shouldn't have done what I did next, but I was burning to share my secret and thought it might help my father at least forget his sorrows for the evening. I showed him my treasure.

"What is it?" he asked.

"We're rich," I said. "The Big House is ours."

"Nonsense," he said, but his curiosity was piqued. He stopped the truck, stared at the key, then took it and weighed it in his hand.

"It's ours, all ours," I said. "You think the key really counts? You think we can keep it? I didn't steal it."

My father turned to me without saying a word. His face was marked by confusion and the clouds that ran over it promised the worst of storms.

"Who gave this to you?" he asked.

"It's his will," I said. "I'm the heiress."

"Who gave this to you?" he asked again, holding the key up to my face. Then he pulled it apart. In one hand he now held the bit, and in the other a corkscrew. "Who?" my dad asked, and I knew better than to keep my silence.

We turned around at once, and instead of driving to the shed where he kept his tools, he drove up to the rear of the Big House. He cursed loudly, closing his eyes and pounding the wheel with his fists. "It was forbidden," he shouted. "Forbidden. You heard it yourself. If word gets out about this. Can you imagine the gossip in our village? The real heir. Johann's brother." Finally he got out of the truck and approached the back entrance; he seemed to have shrunk several inches.

What exactly happened inside I never learned. But when my father emerged again, his face was pale and without expression. He looked around as though he could find neither his truck nor me sitting by the window. For long seconds he stared into the sky, looked at the blooming hedges that surrounded the courtyard, and chewed on his dirty nails. Bruno von Kamphoff had fired him.

On our return that night, my mother first grew quiet after hearing the bad news, then implored my dad to tell her everything. We stood in the kitchen, our dinner was cooking on the hearth, but nobody thought about sitting down at the table. My father wouldn't talk and just kept shaking his head. I filled in my mother, who listened impatiently, kneading her bunched-up apron. "The real heir," she whispered again and again. When I was done, she had become so agitated that she disregarded my father's sorrow, and said, "Erich, they can't just fire you. Your silence must be worth something to them. They can't just throw you away. You've helped them. They should pay you."

I wouldn't stop talking either and bombarded my father with questions. Was the stranger the real heir? Was he the long-lost brother, and where had he spent all these years? My mother stood behind me, with the hope that maybe this was our stroke of luck, that maybe we had found the key to more money, and maybe even a better house. She stood in the kitchen in her simple housedress and waited for an answer just as much as I did, maybe more. She didn't stop me.

My father had never slapped me, and when he did it then, it seemed to do nothing to cool his rage. He wasn't satisfied. Maybe he realized he had hit only his daughter, that he'd picked on the wrong person, but it didn't matter anymore. The frustrations of all the years during which my mother had nagged and harassed him came pouring out, and he grabbed my hair and pulled me this way and that until he pushed my face into the glass door of our kitchen cabinet. He pulled me back, and my skin tore when he drove my face into the shards protruding from the wooden frame like broken teeth. I screamed, and my mother's voice drowned out mine as she begged my father to stop, but he didn't listen. He was at a loss for answers, for words, and how much better did his hand answer what his lips couldn't.

Martin

The mill on the Droste stood north of Hemmersmoor. Fir trees made it hard to spot the hunched building until you were standing right in front of it, and Jens Jensen swore that on Walpurgisnacht, the mill went up in flames without being devoured, and devils and witches had a go at each other. "Martin," he told me, "Martin, such nasty things you can't even imagine." Other rumors also made it worth our while to visit the Black Mill. It was said that the miller had lived in the same spot for over three hundred years. He'd lost his wife and six children, and no one remembered where his grave was located, or if he had ever died at all.

During the Thirty Years' War, Swedish troops had used the mill's mossy wheel to torture their prisoners and make them betray their compatriots and give up the secret locations of food and jewelry. They had also tortured and killed the miller's family, and spared only the miller, badly cut and with a crack in his skull.

In another version of the miller's story, young men masquerading as soldiers had assaulted the family and killed his apprentices. The miller knew the truth, though, and sought revenge.

Half-dead, he had sold his soul to the devil and gained great powers, and whenever a village youth came to the mill, he was lured in by witchcraft and forced to work until his death. His apprentices had been spotted around Hemmersmoor in the shape of cattle or deer. The only way to kill them, the old people taught us, was to club them. Every third blow had to strike the ground, or else the witch or wizard would not die.

In the summers we reenacted the war, and we strapped prisoners to the wheel and made them ride high into the air and downward into the Droste's dark waters. If you knew how to hold your breath, it wasn't too dangerous to ride the wheel, but playing prisoner was nevertheless a punishment. After four or five full turns of the wheel, you'd beg to be released and were all too happy to show the Swedes where you'd hidden ham, bread, and your young daughters.

At first we went quietly about our business, trying not to disturb the miller, should his ghost still haunt the place. Hemmersmoor had long built its own mill south of the village, closer toward the lake, and while nobody had ever seen a customer on the grounds, the Black Mill was said to be in working order. On every visit we found heaps of finely ground grain near the hatches.

Yet after a few long summer days, during which nothing stirred inside the building, we grew bolder and louder. Maybe the old ghost was deaf. Maybe the Black Miller had left the area for good or finally died; he never came out to confront us. At first we might scare a girl by shouting, "The miller, the miller is coming," but they soon learned not to listen to our cries.

As we got older, the last part of our war game became more important. As soon as the Swedish troops stepped out of the woods, they arrested the miller as he was about to do his work. After the torture, they followed the miller to his hideout and raped the women.

It was Karin and Waltraud Brodersen who agreed to stay hidden in the woods behind the mill, where the miller had hidden his family and belongings. They were as plump and supple as their mother, Heidrun, their skin soft and golden. Heike, the oldest of the sisters, felt she was too mature for our game. Instead we asked Anke Hoffmann to play. In the beginning Linde Janeke had come with us as well, but after her accident, none of us boys wanted to have anything to do with her. "She looks as if she's fallen face-first into a roll of barbed wire," Holger said. Anke scolded him. "You're horrible," she said, but still let him kiss her.

Alex Frick was missing too. He had been sent to juvenile prison during the previous winter, and so only Christian, Holger, Bernhard, and I led the girls into the woods. Our game required that boys outnumber girls, but no one wanted to play the Black Miller because he couldn't take part in the raping. He could only watch and wish to have better luck with the draw the next time.

Our voices were still breaking when we raped Karin, Waltraud, and Anke. They giggled when they saw our penises. We spanked their behinds, sometimes whipped them with willow twigs, and on a lucky day might be allowed to fondle their breasts while jerking off.

"How do you kill a witch?" Christian would shout, his voice rising over the mayhem.

"You club her," Bernhard shouted back. He was in love with Anke and took this love out on the girl's white back. "Every third blow must strike the ground, or she'll never die." Anke always died under his hands.

Sometimes we kissed and got entangled and all bunched up, and we came in our pants while the girls were panting. Other days the girls tortured us, pinched our balls, beat us with sticks, burned our asses with cigarettes, or tied us to trees and showed us everything we weren't allowed to touch.

One day in July, after Holger, Christian, and I had reaped the benefits of playing soldiers and still lay in the girls' arms, their soft hair tickling our lips and faces, their warmth heating us up again, we noticed that we'd lost our miller, Bernhard.

It was important for the miller to stick around, and we'd never violated that rule before. It was good to be with the girls, still it was better to be watched while doling out or receiving punishment. It was painful for the miller to stand by, unable to participate, but we endured that role whenever we had to play it, for the sake of our pleasure the next time.

So when Bernhard was found missing, we were enraged. Pulling on our pants, we stumbled out of the woods. He couldn't be far. We shouted, roared, we threatened to break every bone in his body. He didn't show.

It was on that day, after returning to Hemmersmoor and not finding Bernhard at home and not being able to pummel him, that we asked ourselves who exactly was living inside the Black Mill. Bernhard did not come home, not this day nor the next, and by the end of the summer his parents had given up hope. The moor was treacherous and had claimed many lives, and after search parties did not find a single trace of their son, they stopped mentioning his name.

Christian, Holger, and I, though, kept searching. We had

followed our fathers across the peat bog, we had looked at every inch of the moor, but no one had bothered to search the Black Mill. We'd kept our secret. Often we went to the mill, looking for a way in. We searched for a broken window, for an unlocked door, yet the windows were shuttered and the doors wouldn't move an inch. Each time we found fresh grain on the ground, and each time we waited, hoping Bernhard might appear, might come stumbling out of the woods, having been trapped in a fairy-tale slumber. After dark we returned home, our consciences sanded down by our efforts. We had tried.

As the days grew shorter and colder, Christian and Holger lost interest in the mill. Bernhard, Holger said, had left Hemmersmoor of his own accord. "Maybe carnies picked him up," he mused, "or circus people. Maybe he went to Bremen to live as a beggar or a musician. He did play the flute."

Christian chuckled at such ideas. "He's dead. Couldn't stand watching us with Anke, ran off, stepped into the swamp, and whoosh! In a hundred years the peat cutters will dig him up, as fresh as the day he died."

I wasn't convinced by either theory and made the half-hour trip to the mill by myself. What I expected to find in the end I never asked myself, and even if I had, I wouldn't have been able to answer. Perhaps I wanted to find Bernhard and carry him home like a treasure chest. Maybe the legends of the mill brought me back. Slowly the mill became more important than ice skating with Anke Hoffmann. I still dreamt of our afternoons with the girls, still wished to be near them and crawl under their skirts, but as soon as I saw one of them in the village, the spell was broken. We talked for a minute or two, nodded, and went our own ways.

After Christmas that year, I walked through the fresh snow toward the Black Mill. School was out, Holger was seen every day with a different girl and claimed that Christian was making out with the baker's daughter. They didn't have the time to accompany me.

The forest was quiet, and even though the skies were overcast, it seemed bright like our town hall when decorated for a dance. The snow had robbed the woods of all its dark corners. My steps and breath filled my ears.

Where the mill had to be, thin smoke rose over the tops of the trees, and I quickened my pace, gripping my walking stick tightly. Yet before I reached the river, a cat jumped out onto the path in front of me. It was a house cat, but so large was she that I took two steps backward. Her fur was black, her tail as lively as a serpent, and her round face reached up to my belly. She cocked her head as if to say, "You're here again, Martin. I've seen you before."

I remembered the tales of witches and wizards taking on the shapes of animals and haunting villagers, but I had never seen one before. "Who are you?" I stammered.

The cat kept silent but stepped ahead, her big paws sinking deep into the snow. I had trouble keeping up with her. On reaching the mill, the large wheel lay quiet, bound by ice. Only in the middle of the Droste remained a tiny sliver of open water, like a cut that wouldn't heal. If I should vanish from this spot, who would come and look for me?

When I took my eyes off the thin column of smoke coming from the chimney, the cat was gone. Her steps ended at the front door. Christian, Holger, and I had tried many times to force it open and had found it solidly locked every time. Now it stood ajar, tempting me. I pushed it fully open with my stick and entered.

The first room was the kitchen, with an oaken table and eight wooden chairs set around it. The pots hanging above the fireplace were old and dented and impeccably clean. A fire groaned and hissed, and after staring at this strange scene for a few long seconds, I felt the need to take off my coat. Then I shut the door to the outside.

Plates stood stacked on the table, as though someone had taken them from a cupboard but had been interrupted before being able to lay them out. Someone had written a message in the dust covering the dark oak table. "Come to me," it read, and I gripped my stick, which was wet from the snow, with both hands.

"Bernhard?" I asked in a voice barely above a whisper. "Bernhard?"

I followed a narrow hallway. Through an open door I could look into a small bed chamber. Two beds stood there freshly made, it seemed to me. Slowly I walked toward some wooden stairs, turning my head every other second—my breathing was labored and the quiet inside the mill plugged my ears—and yet I couldn't spy anyone.

Cautiously I climbed the stairs, and much as I tried to step without making a noise, the ruckus was terrible. Everyone inside the mill had to hear me. Soon the people living here would discover me and ask what the hell I was doing. I tried to prepare myself for that confrontation, but who would I meet? Had homeless people made the mill their refuge? Had Christian, Holger, and I in our ignorance never noticed that the old mill was indeed inhabited? Convinced as I was that the building had stood empty all these years, the smell of cabbage soup and the fresh linens destroyed this belief. I was no longer sure what I knew, what I should believe, and in the meantime I believed both things—that the mill had been abandoned and empty and that it was still inhabited.

"Bernhard?" I couldn't hear my own voice.

"Is that you?" a female voice said behind me.

I turned and froze. I heard a squeaking noise and only half realized that my throat had caused it. At the foot of the stairs stood a young woman in a white fur coat. Her hair was carefully done, colorful stones glittered in its locks, and she wore tiny sandals with incredibly high heels. She looked like the Snow Queen—most beautiful and terrifying.

"Martin?" asked the young woman. She seemed both surprised and disappointed, and while my heart still beat in my mouth, I slowly realized who stood on the wooden floor below me. It was Anna Frick, Alex's sister. "How did you get in?"

"Where is Bernhard?" I asked stupidly. My fear melted from my bones, but I still gripped my stick violently. At the same time, I understood how young and silly I had to appear in Anna's eyes.

"Bernhard? What are *you* doing here? You have to leave immediately."

I didn't grasp what she meant. "Why? Is the miller around? And why are you here?"

"The miller?" she said with wide eyes. Then she caught herself and said sharply, "It's none of your business. Get lost."

"Where is Bernhard?" I asked again.

"Is he with you? Did you come together?" Then her face suddenly smoothed out and for a moment she was quiet. Then she asked, "Bernhard? The lost boy? Are you still searching for him?"

My face grew hot, and I stuttered, "I . . . I thought . . ."

"That I'm hiding him here?" she mocked me. And my relief over having discovered a known face turned again into fear. Maybe she really knew where Bernhard was.

"Do you know where he is? What are *you* doing here? How did you get here? What kind of coat are you wearing?" Slowly I walked back down the stairs. "Whose cat was that outside?"

"Cat?" Anna asked. "Oh, I'm a witch, you should know," she said and laughed. "Usually she sits on my shoulder."

What happened next I can ascribe to only my fear and the long search for my friend. Anna had made a bad joke, but my nerves threatened to snap, and I didn't comprehend why she would stand in a fur coat and sandals in front of me. "How do you kill a witch?" I said under my breath, and in one desperate move I jumped down the last remaining steps, raised my stick, and struck that fur-clad apparition. But I had aimed badly and hit only her shoulder. Anna screamed, and maybe I knew then what a terrible mistake I had made, but I also feared her loud voice, which would alert the miller to us. I wanted to shut her up. So I hit her again.

Yet in that moment I could hear a car approaching and then stopping outside the mill.

"Oh God," said Anna. She pressed her hands to her head where I had struck her and lay on the ground now. "Oh God," she said again, and her face turned crimson.

And all my fears returned. Anna was a witch, Anna was my best friend's sister, and I had attacked and beaten her. And who was outside? I dropped my stick and ran down the hallway and into the kitchen as fast as I could. I opened the door and was about to storm out into the snow, when a tall figure, clad in dark clothes, blocked my way. But I couldn't stop, ran into him, and together we tumbled into the snow. I was first to get back on my feet and made toward the woods. I ran, ran, a loud voice at my back ordering me to stop. But I kept going, and only after what seemed like an eternity, after I was thoroughly drained from working my way through the deep snow, did I finally stop, turn to make sure that no one was following me, and then drop to the ground. My face was hot and I welcomed the cold, buried my face only deeper in the snow. How long I lay there I don't know, but shame, anger, and fear fought within me and cooled only after a long time.

It was dark around me when I finally got up again and slowly continued on my way home. I was cold and wet, and no matter how fast I walked my teeth chattered and my face stayed numb. How would I explain that I had struck Anna Frick? How could I confess to my father, the *Gendarm*, that his son might have to go to jail because he had assaulted the pub owner's daughter? And this only one year after Broder had drowned in the Droste River? That time I'd been lucky, saved, because of my father's influence, from sharing Alex's fate.

That it had indeed been Anna Frick and not a witch was all too clear to me, but while I trudged home, I slowly gained confidence that I would get away with my crime once again. I wouldn't have to follow in Alex's footsteps and leave the village. Maybe Anna wouldn't tell her dad about the mill, about Martin Schürholz and his attack on her.

When I got back to Hemmersmoor and saw the lights in the windows and the candles on the Christmas trees, which were maybe lit for the last time that year, I breathed more easily. And when I finally sat down at the dinner table and we started eating what was left of the goose, and my mother told me that one day I would freeze to death because of my foolishness, and my dad asked where the hell I had been all this time, I told them about the Black Mill. I hadn't found Bernhard, no matter how hard I had tried. My parents shook their heads, and my sister, Birgit, laughed. "Did you think the Black Miller was holding him hostage?" she asked.

Of my new secret, I didn't speak to them. I didn't say a word about Anna. Mr. Frick never came to our doorstep to talk to my father about the matter. The dark figure I had toppled back at the mill was no ghost or wizard. Only one family in Hemmersmoor owned a sedan that wouldn't quite fit our narrow streets, a black Mercedes, which all children eyed with curiosity and jealousy. I had never seen Rutger von Kamphoff, and yet I knew immediately who was lying underneath me in the snow. And slowly I understood that, as far as it concerned me, it might as well have been a ghost. Rutger wouldn't come after me.

"And did you see a witch come flying out of the smokestack?" my sister sneered.

I bit my lips, shook my head, lowered it, and slowly counted to thirty.

Linde

Käthe Grimm followed the gaze of a howling dog when she was seventeen and ever since had been seeing will-o'-the-wisps, frightful funeral processions after dark, and weddings of the undead, the faces of the bride and groom torn from the bone. We had many ghost seers in Hemmersmoor, but they could be cured by a friend's over-the-shoulder gaze. For Käthe, it was too late, however—no spell could reverse the damage done by a howling dog.

She had been courted by many men in her youth; now, in her late thirties, she was fat, and warts disfigured her once pleasant features. Her strawberry-blond hair looked dull and was thinning. After she paid a visit to the general store or the apothecary, people found it on shelves and counters.

We all knew her middle-of-the-day outbursts, her high shrieks, wide-open and terrified eyes, her fingers pointing this way and that. Yet we didn't see a thing, and we stopped searching. We hardly heard, anymore, her pleading with ghosts to spare her. Still, before crossing her path girls crossed themselves—we did not want to share her predicament. We wanted to get married.

In the summer four of us spent our long afternoons in

Anke's room, clipping pictures of fantastical dresses from the catalogs her mother received by mail. We dreamed of wedding dresses made from brocade and with long trains, of millionaires in sports cars who would glance only once at us before whisking us away to other countries and continents.

Anke turned a thick notebook with hard, black covers into her wedding book. It contained not only a picture of her dress but also photos of wedding cakes, silverware, and tablecloths. She planned every small detail, and we mocked her because she had cut off the heads of the grooms and drawn new ones.

"Looks like Rutger von Kamphoff," I said.

"He's chasing after Anna." Sylvia was the tallest of us and had been the first to get breasts. She'd kissed two boys, while neither Johann nor Torsten had ever asked me again if I wanted to kiss them behind the school or by the river at night.

"It can't be," Anke said infuriated.

"Sure can," Sylvia replied.

"He'll never marry her. Never ever."

"As if you stood a chance."

Anke closed her book and pouted.

When our dreams became too sticky, we ran to the old cloister. The Swedes had destroyed it in the Thirty Years' War and raped and killed the nuns hiding inside. The order had moved to the south, past Bremen, and never tried to rebuild. Among the ruins we played our favorite scenes from "Sleeping Beauty," *Romeo and Juliet*, and *Antigone*, and we loved the tragic endings of the latter, and let Sleeping Beauty die of grief over her prince's sad fate at the hands of a wizard, dragon, or resurrected stepmother.

On our way through the village, Käthe would stammer

about nine dead children playing hide-and-seek with her. She looked more worn than usual, could always be seen eating crusts of bread as if to ward off evil spirits. Sometimes we snuck up behind her and cried "Boo!" then ran off, not listening to her curses.

"Nine dead children," Sylvia said. "And if they really do exist?"

"She's crazy, always was," Anke answered. I had hardly spent any time with her last summer. On the afternoons I didn't spend at the manor, she usually disappeared to meet the boys at the Black Mill. "Nine dead children. Where would they come from?" She never told me anything about those afternoons she spent with Martin and Christian and the others, but now she didn't want to have anything to do with those "stupid boys." She was way ahead of me. "Käthe says they're all siblings." She tipped her finger to her forehead.

"I wonder if she's ever done it," Heike said. She was Heidrun Brodersen's daughter and the biggest of our small group, with large breasts and a belly. Boys were wild about her, God knows why, and we suspected she had done it, since she brought up the topic every chance she got. Her face grew red and her eyes looked expectantly at us. We liked her the least.

"Maybe," Sylvia said. "Maybe when she was our age. Can you imagine her taking off her clothes now?" Sylvia wore a wreath of daisies in her flaxen hair. We'd played "Rapunzel," yet without enthusiasm. It was hot and the skies hung low, and we sat on the remains of the church walls, which were made from large fieldstones, and our arms and legs were glistening with moisture. Little trees and bushes sprouted in cracks and fissures; we could hear the swallows cutting the air around us. We were bored, and we hated Käthe for showing us every day of the week what might happen to us if we stayed in Hemmersmoor. When Anke suggested we arrange a rendezvous for Käthe, it was a done deal.

It wouldn't be hard to give Käthe a letter and convince her that one of the village men had sent it through us. She was fat and ugly and terrified, but the barrettes in her wispy hair and the lace sewn to her shirts spoke volumes. Yet it was harder to decide on her suitor. Who would want to spend a night with Käthe? We had to be inventive.

"Jens Jensen," Anke suggested. "He's ideal. He's a drunk and won't know who he's with anyway. His wife doesn't care if he sleeps around. She'll be safe from him for a day."

"Yes," Sylvia said. "Jensen is a good choice."

Anke with her dark, shiny hair and smooth skin, Anke with her full lips and white teeth, smiled. Smiled and nodded.

"Let's take the apothecary," I said.

"His wife is jealous," Anke objected. "He'll never do it."

"The apothecary," I said. "We'll take him."

Sylvia shrugged. "We can try. But he'll never go for Käthe. We'd have to pretend he's meeting with someone else."

"Heidrun Brodersen," I said.

"Genius!" Heike shrieked, and for once I was happy for her presence. I had not expected her to agree, but she said her mother was ideal. "She's as fat as Käthe. In the dark he won't know it's her until it's too late."

"In the dark?" Anke said.

"It's got to be dark, for sure," Heike said. "Oh boy, it's going to be fun."

Heidrun Brodersen was a good bet. Men loved her, and

rumors crept through Hemmersmoor about nights she did not spend at home and nights her husband spent at Frick's making sure not to return home until after midnight, downing paid-for drinks until he was nearly dead. Yet I wasn't interested in what happened to her or her reputation. I wanted the apothecary. How I would enjoy watching him in the arms of Käthe Grimm. I couldn't wait.

The first task proved to be as easy as we'd anticipated. One morning, when the streets were empty beneath a blue sky that could convince anybody there had to be a world beyond Hemmersmoor, I found Käthe on a bench in the village square. She'd been at the bakery, buying sweet rolls and éclairs, and she sat smiling in the sun, taking a bite from a dry roll, then pushing part of an éclair into her already full mouth. Finally she took a third bite, from the roll again, and her cheeks were ready to burst. Only now did she start to chew, crumbs and flecks of custard raining down onto her shirt. The smile stayed on her lips even as she chewed.

"Here," I said and handed her the letter. "A man gave it to me."

Käthe stared at me, forgetting to work on the rolls and éclair. "Who?" she said.

I waited until she was done spitting and coughing before shrugging. "I can't say." Then I ran off.

The change in Käthe was tremendous. The rendezvous was not until Friday night, three days away, but by that afternoon she was already a different person. She still screamed, still talked nonsense about skeletons and maids milking the beams of cowsheds and potatoes flying through barns like swallows. Yet that first afternoon after receiving the letter, she wore a yellow dress we'd never seen before, a ridiculous rag that didn't fit the color of her skin or hair but which she presented to Hemmersmoor with an air about her as though she were the princess of Egypt.

Our second task was harder, and I tried to get out of it, but since I had suggested the apothecary as our male suitor, Sylvia, Anke, and Heike insisted. I had no choice.

It took me all afternoon to find him alone in his store. His wife, Rosemarie, often served customers who wanted bandages or cough syrup, and for two hours, I stood on the village square and watched Käthe showing off her yellow dress and talking gibberish. My heart wanted to force itself out of my throat, I was tempted many times to hurry home; only the sight of Käthe and her shiny pink skin and dull hair made me stay.

The bell above the door rang, announcing me. From behind the old counter, Friedrich Penck lifted his gaze. Around him glass jars were neatly arranged on dark wooden shelves. The shop smelled cleaner than anything else in our village, as if the foul air and low lives in Hemmersmoor were unable to touch it. If you closed the door and didn't look at Frick's or Meier's across the square, you might have been in Hamburg, or even in a different country.

Penck wore metal-rimmed glasses and stood as erect as a large and curious bird. A strange calm smoothed his narrow face and commanded respect. I never heard anyone raise his voice to him.

He looked sternly at me and said, "Get out."

I shook my head.

He touched his neatly trimmed beard, following its contours with two fingers. "I told you to never come to my store again."

I nodded.

"So what do you want?"

I stayed silent, my face hotter than my hands. The letter I held was soaked with my sweat.

"I will call the *Gendarm* if you don't leave," he said politely.

"I didn't steal," I finally said, and was mortified by the shrill whine of my voice.

"Of course you did. Listen, Linde. I'm sorry about what happened to you, but you can't take things. Leave now, please."

I shook my head again and stepped forward. I thrust the letter onto the counter separating Penck and me. This made him raise his brows. His nose seemed to grow thinner and longer, as if he wanted to smell what was inside the purple envelope.

"What is this?" he asked flatly. "An apology? It's not necessary. Children can be cruel, and I'm sure you thought my creams could solve your problems."

"It's a letter from someone," I croaked. My scars were burning, hot lines cutting my face, fiery red lines that remembered the breaking glass and my face cutting through it, remembered the hand that held my hair and pushed, then pulled back and pushed again.

"From whom?" Mr. Penck said.

"I can't say," I said. "I'm sorry for what I did." My tongue burned as much as my face; I could barely move it. But this needed to be said, my mission depended on it.

Before I reached the door, the apothecary called me back. He'd opened the letter and was putting it into his coat pocket so hastily that he crumbled the purple paper. "Wait," he said again, and met me with a pot of cream in his hand. "I'm sorry too. I might have been too harsh." He pressed the makeup into my hand and briskly turned around, vanishing into the back of the store.

I could hardly breathe and closed my eyes to keep from crying. Last February Mr. Penck had caught me, taken me by the arm, and dragged me to my parents' house. They had looked at each other with sad faces, and my dad had nodded silently. He had paid Penck for the makeup even though I no longer had it on me. Then he'd sent me to my room and never talked about the theft again. He knew the boys were still mocking me. "Mincemeat," they called me.

I held the tub in my hands for a long time. Then I ran out, ran until I reached the Droste. I couldn't think clearly, couldn't distinguish the screams that ran through my head, the twitches within my body. Yet I hurled the pot as far as I could and yelled when it disappeared in the water. I had him. I had Friedrich Penck. He would see, he would see.

Friday night we climbed the walls of the old convent. Our faces were smeared with soot, our bodies draped in grotesque rags. We were the plague, the harbingers of the black death. We hid on what remained of the second floor, where we could see our victims but couldn't be detected ourselves. This second floor was said to have housed the organ, which the Swedes had torn up and carried off. Now only a third of the wooden floor existed, and it wasn't safe to walk on it unless you knew which beams could still carry weight.

We came at twilight, changed from summer dresses into ghoulish costumes, darkened our faces, and took our positions. The sun had not taken the heat with her, sweat smeared our fearsome paint. The air seemed full of wet smoke.

Käthe arrived first, just as we had planned, and just as we had instructed her in our letter, she installed herself in the shadows of the room below. She was muttering under her breath. Even though there wasn't enough light left to see what she was wearing, we could smell her perfume from our high perch. Like lemurs, we hovered above her, watching her dark figure through cracks in the floor. She was a seer, but love had done its job and blinded her. Or maybe all she could see were ghosts, and our bodies were too young, our hearts beating too wildly, for her to detect us.

After fifteen minutes the apothecary approached the convent. We could see him cross the moor, a shadow darker than our liquid night. His feet soon scraped over the stone and steered toward the corner where Käthe was waiting for her alleged suitor.

For seconds I didn't hear a thing, and even if the figures below had moved, I'm not sure I would have been able to hear them above the blood pounding in my ears. It is too dark, I told myself. It is too dark—I will miss out on my revenge. I raised my torso, ready to jump up and leave my lookout.

Just then we heard the apothecary's voice. "Is it really you?" he said.

"Yes," Käthe answered.

Maybe the apothecary understood immediately that it wasn't Heidrun Brodersen who had come, because silence ensued. We couldn't take any chances.

I gave the sign.

A torch lit up in Anke's hand and she dropped it through the floor to the room below us, where dry branches and straw greeted and spread the flames.

"No," Käthe shouted, clinging to the apothecary who tried to tear away from her grasp. "I'm here, I'm here!"

The fire ate its way toward them, and in the unsteady light our faces appeared above the fighting couple. "Lovebirds fly, spread your wings!" we howled. We ran along the walls, screeching and banging frying pans against the stone.

Finally Penck pushed the crying woman away and ran. "Run home to your wife," we yelled and laughed after the fleeing apothecary.

Staggering after him, Käthe shrieked as much as we did. She wore a pink dress, one sleeve torn off from her struggle with Penck. She spun like a top, like a whirling dervish, but she couldn't see us. The afterlife haunted her, but our faces, sooty and distorted, she could not read.

"Käthe," we howled, "Käthe, run after your lover. Run or you'll lose him." We knew we were safe. "Käthe, where is your kiss?" We jumped off the walls and chased after her until we reached the first house of our village.

Käthe stayed hidden for a week, and when we saw her again in the street, words sprang from her mouth like frogs, hopping away in whichever direction, too fast and slick to be caught.

Yet I wasn't satisfied.

I had imagined my revenge for so long, and I hadn't seen Penck suffer enough. I had barely seen him.

For a week, I expected him to show up at our door, insisting to talk to my father, but he never did. Each day, our prank seemed more childish to me, and I was ashamed of the memory of our darkened faces, the silly shrieks, and of how wonderful I had felt as the girls waited for me to give the sign to start the mayhem.

After another week I knew what more I had to do to. Before I left the house that afternoon, I felt my father's hand on my shoulder, turning me around. He traced my scars with one of his thick, rough fingers. "They're red," he said. "What are you excited about?"

"None of your business," I said.

His finger kept running over my face, a spider weaving its web. "If I could undo it."

"Don't worry," I said. "It's all forgiven."

In the village square, people were gathered, their voices high, their mouths watering, and I soon found out what had happened. Käthe had attacked the *Gendarm*, begging him to arrest nine dead children who followed her around all day. She had bitten Mr. Schürholz's hand, and he had taken her away to the station. It was a good moment for my mission, because Rosemarie Penck stood with her nose pressed against the apothecary's window.

The door's bell caused her to abandon her lookout and stare at me in surprise. "What do *you* want? You're a thief, Linde. You're not welcome here."

This time I didn't try to make conversation. I gave her the letter.

"What is it?" she asked.

"It's for your husband," I said.

"From whom?" She turned the purple envelope this way and that, then glanced quickly toward the back of the store. Her fingers already twitched with curiosity.

"I can't say."

Martin

Heidrun Brodersen was a charming woman, fat and gentle and with a way about her that turned heads and caused the men and boys of Hemmersmoor serious heartache. Our mouths were always running, but when she appeared, her big legs stepping as lightly as those of a child, perfume rising from her clothes, we stood silent, as though a deity we couldn't grasp had touched us. One of her ancestors, she claimed, had been burned at the stake for bewitching the village and bringing on a drought. A toad was found at the bottom of the well, just as the dying woman confessed, and once it had been killed, water came rushing back to the village.

Heidrun had three daughters, Heike, Karin, and Waltraud, and we were after them, trying to grope them on their way home from school, pressing our noses against the Brodersens' windows at night, sitting in the trees around their house. If we lucked out, one of the girls, who shared a bathroom on the second floor, would undress in front of us without closing the curtain of the small, slanted window. We liked to imagine they knew we were waiting in the dark and enjoyed performing for us. Heidrun kept large earthen flowerpots on one side of her yard, with rosebushes climbing out of them and spreading over the old stone wall that separated their yard from the Hoffmanns'. Many times, after catching glimpses of bare shoulders and white skin, we broke off a few blossoms and laid them out on windowsills or the front steps.

Only a year ago we had played with the girls in the woods behind the Black Mill, but ever since that summer they had changed. We could see their transformation but didn't comprehend it. Karin and Waltraud wouldn't let themselves be led into the forest anymore. Rather they waited to be invited to the movies or to a café in Groß Ostensen. The apprentices from Brümmer's factory rode their mopeds through our village, and we watched helplessly as the girls got on and put their arms around them. We wanted to appear adult, but we didn't have motorcycles or money. We were left to worship the Brodersen girls from afar.

"Karin, my sweet Karin," Holger murmured, his hands down his pants, his branch shaking. One October night he fell out of the tree, his hand still around his prick, and broke that arm and a leg. We jumped off our own branches and bent over moaning Holger, not able to decide whether he was ecstatic or in serious pain; his face was bent into a grin.

"We could ring their bell and ask for help," Christian suggested.

"And what would we tell them we were doing?" I scolded.

Finally we lifted Holger off the ground and carried him to Dr. Habermann, who cursed us while assessing the damage. "She put a spell on me," Holger later told every boy in school, but that didn't deter him from reclaiming his lookout once the casts were off.

Waltraud was the youngest daughter, and, Christian swore, the one he would marry. I didn't care much for her or for Karin. I was mortally in love with Heike, plump as her mother, with light-blue eyes and heavy breasts. She was seventeen, I was fourteen. Worlds divided us, even though I was already taller than she was.

If I spotted Heidrun Brodersen in front of one of our stores, I went up to her and asked if she needed help with her bags.

"That's nice of you, Martin," she said, and my ears were full of bees. If she knew who pissed in her yard, and who sat in the trees trying to steal a glimpse of her daughters, she didn't let on.

"Your mother says you're doing well in school. She's very proud of you," she said.

I nodded, lifting her bags, hoping none of my friends would see me. Heidrun asked me about my plans for after school, my hobbies, and if I already had a girlfriend, and I stuttered and mumbled, and my face glowed with embarrassment. When I put down her bags at her door, she asked, "You want some water? Some chocolate?"

I nodded yes, then ran off anyway.

Peter Brodersen, Heidrun's husband, was as big and gentle as his wife, but a dullard. He was well liked and a failure. He'd had to sell his farm and, after paying off his debts, went to work as a peat cutter for the new owner.

On nights when people bought him drinks at Frick's Inn, he'd sigh. His heavy face would glow and he'd say that if only his wife had given him sons, he'd still be farming and buying drinks for his friends. "Women," he said. "I'm surrounded by women."

Nevertheless, the Brodersens didn't seem to be in need. The

dresses of Karin, Heike, and Waltraud were new and clean, and Heidrun Brodersen never went out without a hat of the latest fashion, her plump little feet stuck in delicate shoes. She was quite something.

My mother, with hazel eyes that softened her features, had nothing good to say about her. Her house wasn't as clean as it ought to be, she wasn't a great cook, and she seemed too pleased with the impression she made on men. "Who is she dressing up like that for?" she said. Mom herself had rheumatism and bandaged her legs and was the only woman in the village to wear pants. "Who is that woman after?" she asked.

In the winter we abandoned our high perches, and we saw little of Heidrun, who every year around Christmastime grew sick and stayed indoors. After the first snow, should we stand yearning outside the Brodersens' kitchen, watching the family eat a stew or some fried potatoes, we pissed hearts into the flowerpots, each one a sign of our undying love and lust.

Around Christmas Peter Brodersen was always in a foul mood. His wife sick, he was seen all too often at Frick's and, even though he couldn't afford it, drank with whoever was willing to keep him company into the wee hours.

"He's drinking away his daughters' future," people in Hemmersmoor said. The women talked about him in the bakery, shaking their heads. "He's no good. He has a sick wife, three daughters. What is he doing at Frick's all night? He should be at home."

The men in Hemmersmoor sided with Peter. Whenever the women in the bakery got too loud, the baker would come and scold them. "He's a decent fellow," he said. "Thick, yes, but decent. He's the best man Heidrun could wish for." The apothecary, too, had only kind words for Peter. "He has character. Fate has dealt him bad cards, but he doesn't complain." Men and women in Hemmersmoor disagreed, and disagreement focused everyone's eyes on the Brodersens' small house. As for us, the boys, we couldn't have cared less about Peter. We could not fathom how a dullard like him could have produced three daughters like these, and the less we saw of him, the better.

In the spring Heidrun Brodersen reappeared in her garden, planting flowers. She seemed thinner, though not thin, after her long sickness, but she looked as striking as ever. The first time she walked into the bakery, she wore a green hat with feathers and rhinestones, and by midafternoon it was all Hemmersmoor could talk about. Yet something had changed during the winter, and when Heidrun planted a new rosebush in another flowerpot in her garden, people did not stop to chat with her. They did not congratulate her on her green thumb.

With the few hairs sprouting from my cheeks and chin long enough to call a beard, I ran after Heike one afternoon. "Hey," I called out.

Heike turned around. She was a summer landscape in full bloom. She had a boyfriend now, a nineteen-year-old who drove an old Opel and worked at Brümmer's factory. "What is it, Martin?" she asked.

"I . . . I wanted to ask you. You know, the carnival is coming to town soon, and maybe you'd like to go."

Her eyes, so light they seemed to water even at night,

blinked a few times, as though I were so paper thin that she had a hard time seeing me. "I can't," she said.

"You're going with Rüdiger?" I asked.

She smiled. "Yes."

I stepped up to her and, before she could avert her face, planted a kiss on her lips.

"What was that?" she asked.

"A kiss," I said stupidly.

"I'd like to go to a dance," she said. "Why don't you ask me out sometime?" Then she turned and walked away. I waited several minutes before I could feel my legs again. My heart beat in my throat, and I couldn't eat for the rest of the day.

When my mother was told that I had been seen talking to Heike, she sat me down and said that the Brodersen girls were not for boys like me. Heike was too old, too experienced.

Yes, I would have said, exactly, but I heard her out; any opposition would have further raised my mother's voice and prolonged her already long speech. In the evening she told my father. He sighed and said, "Your mother is right. The Brodersens are not bad, but you should not go after an older girl."

"That's it?" my mother said. "That's all you have to say?"

My father, the *Gendarm*, was a bulky man, with red skin and red hair, and his hands, though small, could squeeze all life out of you. "He's young," he said. "He's not marrying her."

My mother gasped and glowered. "You always stick together," she then said. "You and Penck and the others. You buy drinks for Peter so he keeps his mouth shut. Don't think I don't know what's going on."

Maybe our love for her daughters rendered us deaf to the rumors that were widely traded. Maybe the complaints the women of Hemmersmoor had about Heidrun had always been more than gossip, and we had simply not understood their meaning. It might have been jealousy that finally caused the confrontation, or it might have been money, yet what I remember is Heidrun's green hat, the feathers moving in sync with her steps. Whatever it was that upset the fine balance Hemmersmoor had kept, we never felt it coming.

On August 2 the weather was humid and the sky full of lead. Everyone in the village acted nervous, and my limbs ached because I was growing a centimeter every month. A few of us stood in the village square, smoking, when Käthe Grimm bit my father's hand. She was a ghost seer, but in the last few weeks she had acted especially peculiar. One day she appeared in an expensive dress and reeked of perfume, and the next she was screaming about dead children following her every step. Today she had begged my father to arrest the ghosts, and when he finally tried to lead her home—more and more people had gathered to laugh at her—she attacked him.

We were hollering and yelling at Käthe when Rosemarie Penck, the apothecary's wife, came running from her store. She made her way through the crowd to better see what was going on, or so we thought. But it wasn't Käthe she was after. Instead she went up to Heidrun Brodersen in her green dress, took aim, and beat the woman with her purse.

Käthe's screams didn't abate, but nobody except for my dad, whose hand was bleeding profusely, took notice. Mrs. Penck was a small, wiry woman, and we laughed at her efforts. It looked too strange, small Mrs. Penck beating a woman two or three times her size.

Mrs. Penck wore her white coat and gold-rimmed glasses, her already high voice climbed several octaves. "Whore, whore!" she screamed. "How dare you walk through Hemmersmoor like this? How dare you mock the people who've fed you and your children? You whore!"

We held our breaths. With one strike of her fat arms, we expected Mrs. Brodersen to silence her attacker. Nothing like that happened though. Heidrun took blow after blow, and soon her nose bled and sprayed red dots onto Mrs. Penck's white coat. Even then she stood facing the apothecary's wife and waited quietly until her attacker's rage or arms had tired.

The women faced each other, Mrs. Penck breathing heavily, Heidrun touching her nose with the sleeve of her dress. Then Mrs. Penck started crying silently. Heidrun slowly reached out and Mrs. Penck tolerated the fat, small hand on her shoulder. They stood together, and they both cried, and then the apothecary's wife ran off.

When I brought this up at dinner, my mother glared at my father but continued eating her soup. My dad shrugged and wouldn't say what was the matter. But a few hours later, after Mom had gone to bed, he came to my room and said, "Some things are too complicated to be talked about. Heidrun might have done something that wasn't right, but we can't judge her without . . . ," and then he broke off and left.

We didn't see Heidrun Brodersen for two weeks, and we never saw that green hat again. Over the long, hot summer, a new silence spoiled life in the village. You could feel that silence, touch it, when you entered the bakery and stared into the women's faces. You saw it at Frick's Inn, where Peter Brodersen now sat alone, even though a fresh drink appeared as soon as he'd finished the last. But none of the men would pat him on the back or sit next to him. They had to think of their own families.

Maybe the silence grew and widened like the mash in that fairy tale by the Brothers Grimm, until it threatened to suffocate the village. Perhaps Mrs. Penck wasn't the only woman who looked at her husband with suspicion, and more and more often the women of Hemmersmoor stood together in the street, never saying a word. They sweated in the heat, the mosquitoes feasted on them, but they kept quiet.

One day, however, this silence came to an end. Without any new developments, we could suddenly hear Heidrun's name on every corner. First it was like a hum, but each day it grew louder. As soon as we left the house, Heidrun was at the center of every discussion, and the women didn't try to hide their suspicions any longer. They asked why Peter's glasses were refilled as fast as he managed to drink them, and why Heidrun always disappeared from view around Christmas. Their voices could be heard everywhere, and often Heidrun's name was mentioned together with that of Helga Vierksen, whose house we had burned down years ago and whose entire family had been hastily buried in our cemetery.

Heidrun did not enter the bakery anymore; instead her daughters did all the shopping. We waited for them outside the stores, to fight over who would carry their bags. Yet our mothers followed us with eyes full of anger and scorn, and slowly Karin and Waltraud had no one left to help them.

I despaired. Rüdiger, Heike's boyfriend, had a new girl, and I was waiting for my chance. But how could I approach her without angering my mother? At night I lay awake and tried to gather my courage.

Two weeks before school started again, we saw Heidrun for the last time. Summer dragged on like a stubborn and irate mule, and everybody in the village seemed to be waiting for a hurricane or thunderstorm. We looked up to the skies, which hung over Hemmersmoor low and as yellow as sulfur but refused to tear and empty themselves.

Yet no one had anticipated the four policemen who, together with my dad, entered the Brodersens' house one morning to arrest Heidrun. Soon half the village had gathered in the street. The crowd laughed as Heidrun was led from her house in handcuffs. Some taunted her, but nobody understood what was happening when the police made Heidrun sit down in the car and then entered her garden.

One by one they emptied the flowerpots we pissed on during the winter, tore out the rosebushes, and dug around in the soil. The villagers held their breath, and around noon nine small skeletons lay in a neat row on the ground.

Everybody was shocked. Everybody said so. Who knew what questions the police might ask? "Where did the babies come from?" we asked. "How did she manage to keep her pregnancies secret?" We told the police nothing.

"The kids were all by her husband, every one of them," my mother said loudly one evening. "That's what she told them. Why would she lie about such a thing?" Her voice was too shrill and much too loud. It was important to her. My dad nodded.

Two days before the police from Groß Ostensen arrived, I

had asked Heike to come with me to a dance. Fear made me feel nauseated, and I nearly screamed my question, but I got my words out without stumbling or stuttering once. Surprised at myself, I waited wide-eyed for Heike's answer.

Two days after the arrest of her mother, Heike and her father and sisters left for Hamburg. It was said that Peter had a cousin in the city who could get him a job at the docks. That afternoon Christian and I went down to the Droste River and hurled stones into the murky water. Ever bigger rocks we dug with our nails from the mud and flung them into clouds of mosquitoes. I almost hit Christian in the head because my tears blinded me.

Heike had hesitated for a moment before saying yes, and then she had squinted and a smile had opened her lips. I had stared at this small opening and an entirely new fear had gripped me. I had nagged my parents about the dance without telling them who my date would be, and finally they had agreed to buy me a new suit. I had been up all night and asked myself how I could win Heike's heart without ever having had a chance to set foot on a dance floor.

Yet I didn't wear the suit that summer or in the fall, and the following year I had already outgrown it. There was a moth hole in the right sleeve.

Anke

When we were toddlers, Linde and I baked mud cakes in the sandbox behind our house. We learned to ride horses on my family's old mare. I loved Linde so much that instead of looking into a mirror, I looked at her to see myself. We were fifteen during the spring when the beggar woman's curse haunted the village, and newborns and young children were found dead.

Ever since an accident two years before, Linde's face had been crisscrossed by scars, which turned red when she was excited or angry, but her green eyes seemed to glow even when there was no light, as though some invisible admirer was holding a candle to her features at all times. Her nose was large and well formed, her hair a shiny auburn. She was a good student, and her father, who worked as a gardener at the Big House, told everyone that she would go far.

Boys noticed me first though, talked to me first. My parents called me pretty, Jens Jensen blew me kisses whenever I walked past him, and the evening Ernst Habermann kissed me behind my parents' house, it dawned on me that I had outdone my friend. I had discovered new riches, and if I lost my sisterly feelings for Linde, my affection for her intensified. In front of her imploring eyes, I opened my treasure chest to share my new adventures and hang boys' kisses like jewels around my neck.

When Ernst invited me to a dance in July, my mother, more eager than myself, bought me a sky-blue dress and white shoes. I was her only daughter; my three brothers had no need for frills. On Friday night she braided my hair, pulled new stockings from her dresser, and applied rouge to my cheeks and kohl to my eyes.

A stranger stared back at me from the mirror on my mother's dressing table, somebody who looked laughable and breathtaking at the same time. I stood horrified in my parents' bedroom. I feared a false step or a sudden movement of my face would make this apparition crumble. If it had been in my powers, I would have stopped my heart.

My mother embraced me carefully and kissed my hands. She was thin, her back round, and her face drawn. Only our hair had the same dark-brown shade. "Don't waste your time on nobodies," she said in an urgent whisper. "Choose wisely. Only a man you can look up to will do. Don't go for looks, they fade. Your own father wasn't all that pretty, but I knew he'd provide for a family."

"Ernst comes from a good family," I said. "He wants to become a doctor just like his dad."

"Yes," my mother replied, "but be careful. If he takes after his dad, he might look down on you. Your dad has no degree. He's a farmer. Today you're pretty. Today Ernst thinks he's in love with you. But he'll leave our village, and do we know if he'll take you with him?"

"He likes me," I said.

"We'll see how much. Don't agree to anything. Don't spend all you have. You won't be worth a thing once you let him have what he's after."

My mother's warnings were disturbing and yet seemed hollow. This person I saw reflected in her mirror, in the blue dress and white shoes, could have and give everything. Nothing was too good for her, and nothing could be withheld from her.

Before Ernst arrived, Linde came to our house, beaming. "Oh, you're so pretty," she said, stepping away from the door to take a look at me. "Anke, you look . . . old." She giggled, and I laughed too. "All grown up. And look at me," she added. "I'm the ugly duckling." The light in her eyes dimmed for a second before returning. "But guess what? I'll be going to the gymnasium in Groß Ostensen next year."

I tasted the news from behind a smile and tried to decide whether or not I could swallow it without bitterness. "You received the scholarship, then," I said, buying time.

"Yes. Mr. Brinkmann recommended me to the von Kamphoffs, and I'll have to interview with them next week. If I make a good impression, Mr. Brinkmann said, they'll pay for my books and clothes until I graduate."

"Wonderful," I said. "I will lose you, then."

"Nonsense. I'll be still living here. And," she continued, "you'll be too busy with boys to notice." She winked and ran off. "Have fun tonight."

By the end of the dance I had forgotten about Linde. The strange person that had been created in my mother's bedroom was a success, and when Ernst walked me home after midnight, he pulled me into the school playground and hoisted me onto one of the swings. His fingers crawled up my legs like cater-pillars, tickling me and causing me to laugh.

"Am I a klutz?" he asked, his voice suddenly flat.

I jumped off the swing. "Silly you are," I said without thinking. I understood my role without rehearsals.

"Can I try again?" he asked.

"Maybe," I said and ran. He caught me in front of my parents' house and pressed a kiss on my neck. He was hooked, yet my powers depended on a boy's willingness to hand them to me. I was dying for his next move.

On Wednesday Linde asked me to accompany her to the Big House for her interview. I agreed, looking forward to a close look at the splendor of the mansion. I hadn't been to the manor since I was a child, and Mother made me promise to tell her everything about it. How did the new mistress dress? How would she act toward us? Was she still a country bumpkin?

The whole village had been invited to Rutger von Kamphoff and Anna Frick's wedding, but my parents, who hadn't set foot inside Frick's Inn since my brother's death, had refused to attend. "The von Kamphoffs wouldn't have let that girl enter by the back door," my mother said, "if Rutger hadn't filled her belly. What a sly cow." She was right. Anna's belly was so swollen that she looked impossible in her white dress and couldn't even dance with the groom. The old owner of the inn, however, hadn't skimped on a thing and put on the biggest wedding the villagers were able to remember. Every girl in Hem-mersmoor would have sold her soul to be in Anna's stead.

The von Kamphoffs' driver picked us up from Linde's house.

The kids in the street were gawking and pointing fingers. It wasn't often that a car like this made it into Hemmersmoor. Linde was proud and nervous, biting her lips until I scolded her. Blood trickled onto the handkerchief I gave her.

"What are you worried about?" I asked. "Your father has served them well all his life."

"That's the problem." Again a shadow passed over her face. And then she told me about the incident two years before, when she had encountered the real heir in the manor's maze, and how her father had been fired because of her. "And they rehired him only two weeks later," said Linde. "He's afraid they haven't forgotten."

"The real heir. Then the legend is true?" I asked.

"You can't tell anyone about it. Not even your mom and dad. Swear by your own happiness." Her face grew dark, and her scars turned bright red. "Not anyone."

"Your face," I said. "Is that why . . . ? Was it . . . ?"

"Swear it," she hissed without answering my question.

I swore, and she seemed to calm down a bit. But we sweated into the leather seats, too afraid to ask the driver to open a window. He was a young man, no one from the village, and he wore a uniform as black as the car's paint, and a cap.

For the last few hundred meters, the car seemed to float toward the Big House. It stood on the hill the giant Hüklüt had left before sinking and dying in the moor. Even though we knew it was only a legend, it made the mansion all the more impressive. The building was larger than our school, larger even than our church, and instead of red brick the workers had used yellow stone. And just like royalty, we were driven to the front entrance, where the driver got out and opened the doors for us.

We were greeted by an old woman in a maid's uniform, who promised that our hosts would soon be with us. She led us up the steps to the double-winged doors, which alone seemed higher than my parents' house, and from a churchlike hall into a chamber that seemed to serve as a waiting room. The ceilings were higher than those in any house I knew, and the room was four or five times the size of my parents' parlor. Light came rushing in through tall windows.

No sooner had the maid left than a door on the opposite end of the chamber opened and Anna Frick, now Anna von Kamphoff, walked in. She seemed baffled by our presence, and for several seconds stood staring at us as though she were seeing ghosts. Her shirt stood open, and her infant daughter babbled in her arms.

"Oh my," Anna said. "Uh-oh. I think I, darn . . . I didn't . . . Does Rutger . . . ?" Then a slight smile crept over her face, which was rounder than I remembered and pasty. "Hey there. It's Linde and Anke. You must be here for the interview?"

Linde nodded, curtsying, as though we hadn't attended the same school with Anna. "Hello, Mrs. von Kamphoff."

Now Anna's face dropped all expression before exploding in laughter. "It's me, girl, don't you remember me?" She stepped toward us, bobbing her baby in her arms. "She just drank," she explained. "I'm waiting for her to burp." She turned sideways the way mothers do, to allow us a good look at the baby. The girl had wispy blond hair and a face that resembled a potato. My motherly instincts had not been awakened yet, and I found it hard to fathom why Linde's expression changed and her face started to glow as though she had spied a heavenly treasure.

"How lovely," she cried out.

"Isn't she something?" Anna said, and her face became almost beautiful. "You want to hold her? Charlotte, say hello."

I only realized that Anna had been talking to me, not Linde, when she thrust the baby in my arms. I looked at the little thing and cradled it as I had seen Anna do, and the baby stretched out its arms and yelped.

"She's such a charmer." Anna laughed with delight. "She could even charm that beggar woman," she said, before putting a hand over her mouth. "I'd better watch what I say," she explained in a whisper. "The village is all worried after what happened to that girl."

We nodded. The beggar woman had been the talk of Hemmersmoor since the end of winter, and many young mothers were afraid for their offspring. "It's been bad," Linde said.

Anna sighed and switched topics. "I hardly see anyone anymore," she said. "What with the baby and the fine people coming over from Bremen and the dinners. This house doesn't belong to Hemmersmoor at all, it seems. It's its own small world. We make our own time here—but don't worry, I'm not yet one of them." She spoke of her new home in a low voice, as if someone might overhear our conversation. Her feet were bare and pink. "Let me get Rutger," she finally said, and strode out into the hall.

I still held little Charlotte, and I have often wondered why Anna walked away without her child. Was she a bad mother? Or did she just act foolishly, without thought? Again and again I come to the conclusion that her carelessness didn't mean anything. She knew us well—we were from the same village. We were all Hemmersmoor girls and destined to be mothers. Anna didn't suspect that when little Charlotte grabbed my chest and pulled on my necklace, I would cry out and let her slip. Charlotte fell.

Linde gasped, then picked her up and immediately the child began to cry. The more Linde tried to calm her, the more she screamed. Soon the old maid appeared in the door, no doubt alarmed by the noise, and behind her Rutger von Kamphoff and Anna.

"Oh, oh, what is with my little darling?" she cooed. "Look, I'm here." Anna took her baby from Linde's hands and rocked it gently. Yet the screaming got only louder.

Anna carried her daughter to a table in front of one of the tall windows and sang, "Are you wet, my darling Charlotte, are you wet?"

I thought the scare was over and breathed calmer, but just as Rutger turned to Linde to introduce himself, Anna shrieked, "What happened?" As though she'd been bitten, she took a step away from the child. Charlotte's left arm hung at an awkward angle, lifeless it seemed.

"What happened?" Anna turned on us, demanding an answer.

What I did next altered who I was and who I would become. I broke out in tears, and from behind those tears I saw Ernst Habermann coming to my door to pick me up for a dance. Would I have to tell him? And how would I describe the Big House to my mom without mentioning how I had disgraced myself? Already I saw her face darken with disappointment.

When my mouth opened to find words for my sin, only one appeared clearly in my mind. Just one, and I knew by some dark instinct that it was the right word. "Linde . . . ," I said, then nothing else.

If I tried to talk to Linde on the way home, or if she addressed me, I cannot say. It seems we were in the car for a long time, and in my memory I don't hear a sound. I stared out the window, keeping my eyes from venturing to the left, where Linde sat shrunken in her corner.

I've lost all memory of whom we passed or who was working on the peat bog or in the fields. I recall only the yellow light, thick as honey, and my legs sticking to the brown leather seats. I remember that drive as though we went too fast for me to hold on to a single thought, although speed on our backwater roads was hardly possible. Linde hadn't protested, too perfect had my pitch been. After all, she was holding the baby when Anna entered, and how could she deny my accusation? Any words she might have spoken in her defense would have sounded hollow, would have made her case only worse. She must have understood, for she kept her silence. I was afraid of that silence, but it didn't enter my mind to apologize. I didn't want to trade places with her.

I was dropped off at my house; the chauffeur held open the door. Then Linde, without looking my way, disappeared from my view. In the evening I went to her house, but her mother said that Linde felt sick and was asleep. She avoided me for the rest of the summer, and as my bad conscience was slowly undermined by Ernst's show of affection, I resigned myself to my new adult role. Love was still new.

Linde and I might even have become friends once again had the fall not brought new changes. In October Mr. Brinkmann took me aside and said that I had been awarded the von Kamphoff scholarship, Rutger von Kamphoff himself had intervened on my behalf. Mr. Brinkmann told me that my heartfelt sympathy for my friend's failure and for Charlotte's accident had touched the young heir. He had requested to see my grade sheets and regarded me as an ideal candidate. Here Mr. Brinkmann broke off and cleared his throat. I didn't need to see the bright smile on my mother's face to know that the teacher's words hinted at bigger, still unthought and unsaid, promises.

I accepted the scholarship. It was lost for Linde; I couldn't see any benefit in forgoing the opportunity.

Linde

The New Year bore down on Hemmersmoor, freezing shut the Droste, and our fathers could no longer sail the many canals of the peat bog. Last summer Heidrun Brodersen had been arrested, and her house still stood empty. "A child murderess," the people in our village had lamented. "Who would have thought?" Yet in the meantime they had found a new topic and asked themselves who had ratted Heidrun out to the authorities. Klaus Schürholz had given her up, some said, to silence his wife. At least two of the children had to be his. And Rosemarie Penck, the apothecary's wife, was also a prime suspect. It was she who had hit Heidrun in the face and called her a whore in front of a crowd in the village square. It had to be Rosemarie—she was the traitor. Whenever my mother and her friends discussed this question, I nodded without opening my mouth or contradicting them. Rosemarie Penck. Of course. There was no doubt.

These same friends also reported that you could hear peculiar noises inside Heidrun's house, and our neighbors swore they had seen lights on the upper floor. I laughed at the women, my throat constricted and hoarse. It couldn't be. How could they believe these rumors? I didn't believe them. I didn't want to believe them.

Our neighbor's daughter, Ilse Westerholt, was sick with the flu when the year changed, and her recovery was slow. I had never had any siblings, but Ilse had treated me like a sister, and so I didn't heed my mother's warnings and ran over to Ilse's house to keep her company. Her sister, Irene, slept in the attic, so she wouldn't have to suffer through the same agonizing weakness, and we had the bedroom to ourselves. And there I was safe from the gossip about Heidrun Brodersen, because in Ilse's mind the murders were just too awful; she couldn't talk about them. Instead she made me carry up books from the living room, and when I read to her about the werewolves, as the citizens who had defended their families during the Thirty Years' War were called, she stuffed a pillow in her back and listened intently.

"Red hair?" she said about one of the heroines of the tale. "Oh, Linde, how I would love to have red hair. But no freckles. Freckles are provincial." She screamed in delight when one of the women took up arms and joined the battles. She waved with her arms, clenched her fists, and cried, "That's it." I was almost fifteen, Ilse nineteen, old enough to be married. Her father wanted her out of the house, but he had no dowry to offer, no land to spare, and he had made up his mind to hand her over to some poor devil.

Ilse was thin and her hair was as black as soot. Her skin was white and soft, and she complained every day about her large hands and feet. "Ladles," she said and spread her long fingers in front of my face. They were rough and red from work in the garden and kitchen, and every night she rubbed creams and balm into her skin. Every morning Ilse forced her feet into the tiniest shoes and suffered the pain; she didn't want to look like a clown.

Her heart beat for Rutger von Kamphoff, and his for Ilse. Yet his parents owned the Big House outside of Hemmersmoor; they were rich farmers and had different plans for their firstborn. Before her illness, they'd met on the moor every week, and now she hadn't seen him in twenty days. The rumors that Rutger had a new girl every time he came to the village had never bothered her, but the longer she had to stay in bed, the moodier she became. She had dark shadows under her eyes, and her skin had a greenish shimmer.

One night not long after Epiphany, when her parents were out visiting a neighbor, the doorbell rang. I had read to Ilse, as usual, and now shouted for Irene, who came down the stairs to see who was at our step. Very soon after, she poked her head into the room and said, "Just a beggar woman with her two children."

"What did she want?" Ilse asked.

"Don't be stupid," Irene replied. "She said her children were cold and they were looking for a roof over their heads for the night."

"Did you open the barn for them?" Ilse asked.

"I sent them away. Mother and Father are gone. I can't decide such things."

After Irene left, Ilse and I hurried to the window, but although the night was clear, we couldn't see the woman. "We should have offered her something warm to drink and let them sleep in the barn," she said, yet just the few steps to the window had exhausted her. She felt dizzy and her knees buckled.

Two nights later she sent Irene to the manor house with a message for Rutger, then wrapped herself into a thick wool coat, and even though her forehead was still burning hot, she ran out onto the moor, waiting for her lover. The weather had changed again, snow was whirling around her, and she couldn't see but a few yards in front of her. Her heart was beating as if it wanted to jump right out of her chest and kill her. She waited at their old meeting place for an hour; then the cold drove her away and back to the village.

She berated her sister on her return, but Irene assured her she had given Rutger the message. Ilse slapped her face until her eyes were running and her cheeks a deep crimson. Ilse called Irene names and tore out strands of her hair; still the younger sister claimed to have passed on the letter.

When the snow thawed at the beginning of February and the river once more moved our fathers' boats, Jens Jensen found a woman and her two children frozen to death inside the ruin of the old cloister. It was the beggar woman Irene had sent from her door when she needed a place to sleep, and as news of Jensen's find spread throughout the village, everyone gave reasons why they had not allowed her to warm herself and her children by their hearth. Everyone nodded and accepted any explanation given, because what else could they have done? They had all sent her away. They'd all had good reasons.

The news of the beggar woman's death afflicted Ilse. When I stepped into her room, she only stared glumly ahead. When I read to her, she offered no comments and didn't pay any attention to the heroines' dresses or deeds. What had happened to Rutger? Why hadn't she received a note from him?

Finally she heard from Rutger, but she didn't get a letter with a dried flower and words that jumped off the paper and begged her heart to dance. She didn't get a note saying how much he wanted her to come out onto the moor. Instead, one morning at the bakery, Gertrude Böttcher broke the news to the women buying their bread and pastries and jams and ordering cake for the weekend. "He's marrying Frick's daughter. Not what his clan had hoped for, but the dowry's good. They'd also better hurry with the wedding, or she'll look like a cow in a white dress." Ilse and I stood with all the others in a circle around her.

The women of Hemmersmoor clucked and screeched. The wedding was news, good news, and Anna Frick's shame of carrying a child beneath her heart before the wedding added spice to the dreary February days of sleet, slosh, and faded colors. Over the din in Meier's bakery, no one but me noticed how quiet Ilse had grown, how all blood had left her skin, how the doubts she'd collected for over a month now weighed her down. When we left the bakery, she looked as pale as death itself, and two days later she was bedridden again, this time until the crocuses started to show their gentle heads.

The beggar woman had been buried weeks ago, quickly and unceremoniously, but Jens Jensen, who, because he'd found her dead, now considered himself an expert on the matter, claimed her death was a bad omen and that Hemmersmoor should be prepared for tragedy. Of course, Jensen always expected bad things to happen, and if one of the men bought him a drink at

Frick's, he'd spool off any number of bad omens he'd observed during his long days on the peat bog.

In March we learned that the wedding would be held in June; Rutger and Anna's child was expected the month after. Even Ilse and her parents had received an invitation. She showed the card to me, letting her finger glide across Anna's name. "Can you imagine this?" she asked. "She'll now become the mistress of the Big House." Yet she seemed to be doing better. She appeared again in the streets of the village and inside Meier's bakery. She held her head high.

I suspected nothing. I had not the slightest shimmer of what Ilse had set out to do. The preparations must have been the ugliest part. Yet to taste revenge, you mustn't care about the smell of its ingredients. Rutger's betrayal had devastated her, but now that she was herself once more, she also understood the advantage of their secret relations. No one in the village pitied her or harassed her with questions about her heart's well-being. Ilse's heart had been awakened, then strangled and finally cut out, yet there were no stains, no wounds, no evidence for curious gazes. During her sickness, the chores around the house had been left to Irene, who complained a great deal, but even now that she was no longer confined to bed, Ilse feigned weakness and dizzy spells to preserve her freedom.

Rumors started. The beggar woman's ghost had been seen near the Droste. And when a little girl was found dead but untouched days later, the village was alerted to a new and grave danger.

The girl's death had started a fire, now the villagers smelled smoke everywhere. Before the old doctor's granddaughter was stillborn, neighbors wanted to have seen a gigantic black shadow hovering over the house. "It was the beggar woman," the baker's wife knew. Others saw cows, colts, and cats visit houses and farms after dark, and animals were clubbed to death to exorcise the beggar woman's spirit.

By the time of Rutger's wedding, the village had accepted the burden of the beggar woman's curse. It was upon us, and no one knew how to lift it. When women felt the hour of giving birth draw near, they sent for the priest, yet even his presence could not ensure the safety of the newborn child.

One night in early spring many of us had gathered in Martha Dinter's bedroom to assist her in childbirth. Her husband had been thrown off a horse and could be of no help. I boiled water and gave Martha fresh towels. Ilse assisted the midwife, and an hour after Martha's boy had been lifted into the air and given his first scream he was dead, his face blue, his tongue swollen. "The beggar woman!" Martha cried out. "The beggar woman." And the shame of having refused to help a mother and her children buried any doubt, any suspicion that might have led us to investigate the baby's death. "We are victims of our own wrongdoing," said Ilse, her arms and forehead still bloodied from that night's birth. She looked tired and happy.

My family, too, had been invited to the wedding, the only day I recall that Frick's Inn closed its doors to thirsty workers and farmers, and the first time the von Kamphoffs came to Hemmersmoor to celebrate. Many stared with hostility or bemusement at the chauffeur who held open the doors and the family that extracted itself from the black car that seemed too long and too wide for our streets. I accompanied my parents and saw Anna and Rutger open the dancing that night, and just like everybody else I saw how the new life inside her belly made her dress bulge. Right after she took the first steps, the bride had to be led back to her table; her burden was that heavy. Ilse sat next to her parents and refused to dance that night. Not once did she take her eyes off Anna.

Anna moved into the Big House, where she soon gave birth to a girl. Her husband, with a trusted steward and plenty of hired help, kept close watch over his new family, and no one in the village was able to catch a glimpse of them. Yet during the last days of summer, I received word from our teacher, Mr. Brinkmann, that I would be awarded the von Kamphoff scholarship. For a few short days, I forgot the scars that ran over my face. This was my happiest time in Hemmersmoor, a time when I believed I would escape the village. I wanted to warm myself in the glow of the Big House. I wanted to study and step out into the world. I didn't want to share Ilse's misery anymore. Yes, Rutger had betrayed her, but his family would pay for my studies. Ilse had failed to win Rutger's heart, she would never move into the manor house, but I would be a welcome guest there. I would leave behind Anke and stupid dresses and bows and her saucer-eyed admirers.

For a few short days, I seemed too tall for the low houses in our street. I was able to look down on Ilse and Anke and all the women and men in our village square. For a few short days, I was somebody special.

Then when Anke betrayed me, my world imploded, and when she was offered my scholarship, I knew that I would never leave Hemmersmoor. I still remember our drive home. Every sound seemed amplified, and I can still smell my cheap perfume and the leather of the hot car seats. I saw the green and brown fields, the hard grasses along the road, and I saw how my life was suddenly cut in two. Here I sat, Linde Janeke, on my way back to the village. Full of rage, shame, and without the least bit of hope that I might leave Hemmersmoor. And in another car that looked exactly like ours sat another Linde, whose return to the village was only the start to a new life, a life in which she would travel to foreign cities and countries, a life that lay even beyond her father's dreams. I could see this other Linde, feel what she felt, but then she waved at me and slowly receded, very slowly, until she was driving alongside our car and turned right at the next intersection, onto the road to Groß Ostensen, and disappeared quickly from my view. I've never met that other Linde again.

In the fall I didn't go back to school. In the eyes of my parents I had heaped shame on them once again. My father didn't dare show his face at the manor anymore and found work stocking shelves in a grocery store in Groß Ostensen. Toward evening he left our house in his old truck and returned early the next morning.

While he slept and everything had to be quiet inside the house, I went to see Ilse and spent my days with her. She was the only friend who would still talk to me, and our misery brought us close again. I hadn't wanted to share her misfortune any longer, but now I shared mine with her, and she seemed to welcome my company. Both of us had been betrayed by the Big House and by Rutger.

Anke I saw only from afar. I wanted to break her neck, tear out her brown hair, cut her skin with glass shards, but as soon as

I saw her in the street, I lost all courage. In those moments I myself believed that I had dropped Anna's small girl.

Yet Rutger I hated even more. It was he who had readily believed Anke's lie. It was he who had dropped me after all the years my family had worked for his. Rutger and Anna had sealed my fate. They had betrayed me.

"Wouldn't it be marvelous if you could take revenge?" Ilse asked one day.

I had no hope. What could I do against the von Kamphoff family? "But how?" I asked.

Ilse sighed but didn't reply.

In the fall she took me out into the fields, where kids were flying their kites. "They look so pretty," my friend said. We watched them until dusk, until even the last straggler took his kite and went home. When one of the boys passed by us, he looked at us curiously.

"Hi there," Ilse said.

The boy stopped, but didn't say a word.

"Are you afraid of us?" Ilse laughed.

The boy stuck out his tongue. "You are stupid," he said. "I'm not afraid of you."

"Why are you on your own? Aren't you afraid of the beggar woman's curse?"

The boy took a few steps back. "My father says you're a spinster. And you," he told me, "you are a thief and so ugly that no one wants you." Then he ran off as quickly as his legs would carry him.

I was wearing my father's clothes, his heavy boots, his hat. Ilse had insisted. "He mustn't recognize you. He'll think you're a man." She smiled at me, said how happy she was to have me by her side. "I'm afraid of his rage. If I were by myself, he might harm me." She had sent Rutger a message asking for one last meeting. She had threatened to visit the Big House should he fail to appear on the moor at the agreed hour.

"What will you tell him?" I asked Ilse.

"He only has to listen to me. I haven't had a chance to talk to him in all these months. It's as though we'd never met. But he should hear that I haven't forgotten him."

Despite the cold November night, I was sweating in my father's heavy clothes, and my feet slid around in the large boots. "If he recognizes me, he'll make my parents' life a living hell."

"Just keep your distance," Ilse said. "But I need your eyes and ears. You shall be my witness. Just make sure he doesn't hurt me."

We were early, but as soon as we arrived at our meeting point, a dark figure came rushing toward us. My heart hammered terribly. How could I keep Rutger from harming Ilse? Only then did I fully realize how stupid I had been to follow my friend onto the moor.

Yet it wasn't Rutger who approached us. With bafflement I recognized that it was Anna, who walked toward us with a bundle in her arms. Her coat was made from fur, her boots from shiny leather. On her head she was wearing a round fur hat, and her gloves were thin and elegant.

"What is she doing here?" I asked Ilse, but she motioned for me to keep quiet.

Anna didn't seem afraid of Ilse, but when she noticed me, her steps slowed. "Who's that?" she asked.

"A friend," Ilse said. "He has to help with the magic."

Now she came close, and I saw that the bundle she was bearing was her daughter, Charlotte. "I've worried myself sick since the shadow of the beggar woman was seen over the Big House. It's so scary. All these small children. They are not to blame." She was cradling sleeping Charlotte.

I had no idea what was happening. Magic? What did I have to do with the curse of the beggar woman? What did Ilse claim to know about it? Confused, I stepped closer to the two women, and when Anna looked up from her daughter, she barked, "It's you?"

"I . . . I didn't . . . ," I stuttered. This was the first time I'd seen Anna since that fateful summer day at the Big House, and no words would come. "It wasn't me. It wasn't me," was all I could say.

Anna looked at me in exasperation. "What a bunch of hogwash," she said. Yet before Anna could turn away, Ilse stepped forward, tore the fur hat from her head, grabbed her by the hair, and pressed one of her large hands over Anna's mouth. The girl dropped her bundle, flailed her arms, but even though she tried to fight off Ilse, she couldn't make a sound.

"What are you doing?" I shouted in fear. "What does that mean?"

Ilse didn't reply. She put both hands around Anna's neck and squeezed. A pained moan escaped Anna's throat. Her legs buckled.

"Stop it!" I yelled. "Stop. You'll kill her."

"Not me," Ilse said.

Charlotte cried. She shook her little arms and soon began to scream. When Anna's movements slowed, I started to hit Ilse and demanded she let go. I pulled her hair until she finally dropped Anna to the ground.

"What have you done?" I bent down and looked at Anna's red face. She was gasping for air, too weak to get up. Ilse stood above us and breathed heavily.

"What has she done to you?" Still I didn't comprehend.

Ilse looked at me as if I had lost my sanity. "You have no choice."

"I haven't done anything."

"If you don't do it, she'll run back to the manor and tell on us."

"I haven't done anything," I yelled. "What do you want from me?"

"You are a thief and so ugly that no one wants you. Who will believe you? You have killed them all. The small girl by the river, Martha Dinter's child. You killed them."

"That wasn't me," I screamed, but when I saw Anna starting to stir and regain conscience, I knew how bad my position was. While I pinned her to the ground, I knew that I would never let go of her again. While I pinned her to the ground, Ilse went in search of a rock.

How Rutger's face changed when he bent over the lifeless body and saw what Ilse had done. He had come at the agreed hour; I had failed to run away. Dazed and full of fear, I watched as he got up.

Ilse shook the child in her arms, and it started to cry again. How his eyes gleamed, how rage and fury twisted his limbs. Yet he had to tame himself—she was holding his daughter.

I don't know how long they stood like that. My lips trembled, my teeth chattered violently, and the November cold paralyzed my limbs. Even if I had been able to form a clear thought, my legs wouldn't have carried me away. "What is my revenge worth if I can't share it with anyone?" Ilse had said. Tears were streaming down my face, and I crouched unnoticed on the ground.

Before Rutger could seize Ilse, she broke the little girl's neck. It took Rutger a moment to understand, and for a moment I believed that she had broken his spirit too. But then I watched how rage overcame him, shook him, how his eyes stared at her and how his gaze got stuck in those eyes as though he would never be able to extract her image from them again. Ilse waited, dangled the dead child in front of him.

She didn't run. She took all his rage and let him ravage her. But I ran, ran for my life. As soon as Rutger gripped her, I jumped up and ran back toward the village, ran until the air burned like fire in my lungs. I lost one of the large boots, my father's hat flew off, but never did I look over my shoulder.

In quiet moments I am shaken with disgust for myself, and I grow afraid of my mirror image, which glows pale and looks inquiringly at me as though I were but a reflection. So we often stand for minutes, gazing at each other, until dark sounds rise up inside me, scratch my throat, and open my lips. Then the woman in the mirror hushes me with one gesture of her hand and a furious stare. I avert my eyes.

Martin

They were married young: she fifteen and the daughter of the poor widow Klein, he seventeen and an apprentice at Brümmer's factory. At their wedding my father wore his uniform and told everyone who would listen that Olaf Frick had only his dick for a brain and would surely ruin the family.

Olaf was drunk with love for Hilde—her flaxen braids; the red spots his fingers left on her supple arms; the tiny, almost translucent fuzz at the nape of her neck; and a spot only he was allowed to see. At work he dreamt of her sturdy legs, at night he tried to squelch his desire, but however tired he was in the morning, however often he yawned at work and went outside to have a smoke along the railroad tracks, his desire could not be extinguished.

Olaf was Frick's firstborn, but he wanted nothing to do with the family's inn. He didn't enjoy talking to patrons, didn't enjoy serving them. He hated sweeping and mopping and waxing the pub's floors after closing. He would earn his own money; he would take the silver spoon from his mouth and work his way up. His father, Bernd, shook his head—such ingratitude. But he had personally talked to Otto Nubis, the foreman of Brümmer's factory, and put in a good word for his son.

Olaf was let go when his drowsiness cost Jan Hussel his left hand. He rode the ten kilometers to Groß Ostensen on his bike and visited Jan and tried to apologize, but Jan did not want to hear what Olaf had to say.

"It's your fault, Olaf, no matter how sorry you are. Look at this hand!" He held up the bandaged stump, blood still seeping through the white gauze. "You think my wife wants me to touch her with that? Do you? So when you go home to your Hildchen, think of that hand. I wish it had been yours."

Olaf's money, and whatever little Hilde brought home from helping out on one farm or another, had been enough to support them in their own little place, a heap of stones that once had been the gatehouse to the von Kamphoffs', long before the Big House was built. It stood on the moor, a kilometer from Hemmersmoor, and come January, no matter how hard you looked around the snow-swept landscape, you couldn't find the place.

Work was scarce, his reputation shot, and after a few months of living off his parents' goodwill, Olaf's father took him aside. "It's time you thought of your wife," he said. Bernd Frick was a head shorter than his son and his movements slow, as though weights were pulling at his arms and legs. He was nearly sixty and held himself erect. He still worked every day behind the bar, and if not for the generosity he showed toward Otto Nubis, his son would never have been hired in the first place.

Olaf was at a loss for an answer. He knew his father felt responsible for what had happened to Jan and wanted to make things right. "What should I do?"

"You can start here again whenever you want. It's your inheritance."

Olaf nodded quietly. It all seemed so easy. But then he said, "I can't do that. Especially after what just happened."

Bernd sighed deeply, he hadn't expected anything different. "Then you need to leave."

The next week Olaf left Hilde with his mother and father in Hemmersmoor, and went to Hamburg to look for work. He'd save enough money to furnish a place, then send for his wife.

Alex and I were ten years old when Olaf left the village, and we didn't pay him any attention. Alex loved the inn and often kept his father company behind the bar. He stole liquor and cigars for us, and we watched his sister through a crack in the floorboards whenever she smuggled a boy into her room.

Slowly news from Olaf began to arrive. The first few months were rough for him. He slept in a flophouse, worked at the docks when help was needed, but couldn't save enough to even think of supporting a family. Then he took a chance and signed on as a sailor on a freighter going to America. He did not have time to visit Hilde, only sent her a letter explaining that he would be back within a few months. The message informing him of his mother's death arrived at his former dwelling just as the *Brunhild* reached the open sea.

Bernd Frick was now wearing a black suit every day, and when I arrived at the inn to pick up Alex, he didn't seem to notice me. Before his wife's death, he'd sometimes pour me a glass of soda, but nowadays he only smiled absentmindedly.

From New York, Olaf sent another letter to Hilde. He wrote that he was leaving for Buenos Aires. He missed her, dreamt every night of coming back. He hoped it wasn't too hard on her, staying with his parents; he knew how his mother could be. He'd be back with his pockets full of money. She would see.

Yet he didn't come back from Buenos Aires either. Colorful postcards from Cairo, Vancouver, San Francisco, and Macao reached Hemmersmoor, where the mailman showed them around at the bakery.

"Don't read it," he warned the baker's wife. "But look at that city. I didn't even know that place existed."

During the first two years of Olaf's travels, the neighbors often asked about him. Yes, the accident at the factory had been a terrible thing, but was it really necessary to stay away so long? Where was he now? What did Hilde know about his whereabouts? Maybe he had sent a picture?

After two years the questions became more infrequent. And Hilde's answers grew ever more terse. Yes, he was still writing to her. Yes, he would return soon. But after five years, Olaf still had not come back to Hemmersmoor, and slowly people forgot about him. Hilde lived with her father-in-law, helped him around the inn, and ran the daily errands. Sometimes, after she left the bakery, Mrs. Meier said, "What a shame. Such a young, beautiful girl."

The Fricks, the wealthiest family in the village, found no peace. First Alex was sent to juvenile prison; then Anna married Rutger von Kamphoff and became the main source of village gossip. All eyes were on her wedding. Such a spectacle had never been seen in Hemmersmoor, and the villagers whispered that the von Kamphoffs needed Frick's money to stay afloat. But half a year later, Anna was dead, and Rutger von Kamphoff stood trial for manslaughter. Nobody in our village had time for missing sailors.

After seven years Olaf finally came home. He was twenty-five, broader in the shoulders, with a harshened face and a mustache. He wore a peacoat and carried a canvas bag on his back and a new, shiny leather suitcase in his left hand. He looked taller too, the women of Hemmersmoor remarked. Mrs. Hoffmann sneered. "He must be a beast after all the years in those dark countries." She had never forgiven the Fricks for her son's death.

Olaf walked straight to his parents' house, where for the first time he learned of his mother's death. Jan Hussel's accident had been the harbinger of only worse tragedies. Bernd Frick was a rich man, but his children had brought him only shame and disappointment. Some people claimed that the family was star-crossed; others said Bernd had been a bad father and spent too much time emptying our pockets. But maybe Olaf's return would change the family's luck. Alex had been released from juvenile prison and every night, after closing, helped at the inn. The house was clean, and Bernd Frick, though older, in good health.

And there was Hilde. Olaf felt dizzy watching her. She had filled out—the young girl he knew had turned into a woman. She was his wife, and what an odd idea that had to be. All these years he must have hoped to get back, and here she was now, and it was quiet in his father's living room. She embraced him, whispering, "You look so strange."

Olaf had big plans. He had spent little of his money and saved enough to build his own house. He wanted to run his own business, maybe take over the boat-repair shop from Peter Falkenhorst or sell motorbikes in Groß Ostensen.

This he explained to us in his father's living room, while eating stew Hilde had cooked. "You could have let us know you were coming," she scolded. My parents and my sister, Birgit, plus the Fitschens from next door and the Meiers with their daughter, Sylvia, had come to look at the trinkets Olaf had gathered on his travels. He showed us a blue scarab. "What an odd thing to worship," Sylvia said, and turned the bug in her hand. Olaf showed us a stone Buddha he'd bought in Shanghai, masks from Africa, and a brass figurine of what he said was the Statue of Liberty in New York.

Our families shook their heads—wasn't it peculiar that those foreign peoples should make such strange-looking things? What did they need a dance paddle for? Who had ever heard of dancing with a paddle?

Later, after the Meiers had gone, Bernd Frick opened a bottle of Bommerlunder, and Olaf started to discuss his plan of building a new house.

Bernd Frick's hair was white now. His belly protruded over his pants, and lines had sunk deep into his face. And yet, sitting together, the sailor looked like a younger, taller version of his father, his features only softened by his mother's prettiness. Even after years at sea, a certain softness remained around his mouth and eyes, one that Bernd and Alex entirely lacked.

"So where are we going to build it?" Olaf asked.

His father waited a few seconds before shrugging. "You might already have a plan."

Olaf smiled. "I thought we should build upriver, right by the Droste. We'll be close to the village, and if I should go into the boat business, I can expand right there. What do you think?"

Alex grunted approvingly. He was wearing a mustache now and was almost as big as his father. "Sure thing. I can help you."

"We're all going to help," my parents agreed.

The elder Frick thought for a while. "It's a good plan. And yet . . ." He folded and unfolded his hands. "You know, after your mother's death I realized that I won't live much longer either. I'm nearly seventy, and I might still have a few good years in me, but at some point not too far off in time I'll die and you, as my only son, will inherit this house." He sighed.

Alex frowned at his father's remarks. He hadn't missed his brother, and even though there was no bad blood between them, he didn't like the prospect of Olaf eventually taking over the inn. His father didn't like Alex to show his face at the pub, out of fear that the villagers still bore him a grudge over Broder Hoffmann's death. But once enough time had passed, Alex intended to manage the inn.

"When Helga died," Bernd Frick continued, "it was hard on me. She'd been my companion for thirty years. Without Hilde, the house would have fallen apart and I myself with it. What do you say? Why don't you young people add on to this house, and once I'm gone it's all yours?"

Olaf chewed his lip. His parents' house was close to the village square, and he did not like the thought of being scrutinized by his neighbors and providing fodder for their gossip. Still, he had missed his mother's funeral and felt an obligation to keep an eye on his father. "I'll think about it," he said and put an arm around Hilde, who had listened to the conversation without saying a word. "You're hurting me," she said and squirmed. He laughed. "I'm a klutz. I'll be more careful."

Early next morning I ran to the village square, hoping to meet Olaf alone and ask him about the ships he had worked on. I wanted to know how he'd felt, traveling the world all by himself, how big his ships had been, and what he had seen in the different ports. I had heard of Bombay, of Baghdad and the caliphs, but so far they had existed only in fairy tales. Olaf had seen these cities with his own eyes. What stories he might tell me.

I had another reason to wait for Olaf, however. After last night's talk, I was hoping I could work for him and save enough money to buy a moped. I had never done construction but was convinced I'd be able to persuade him.

When Olaf finally appeared on the terrace of the inn, his hair was wild, and he squinted into the daylight and looked around as though our square was the most peculiar place on earth. I said hello, and he didn't seem to recognize me at first. Then he shook his head and said, "Martin. I was just about to take a little walk."

"Can I join you?" I asked.

We walked along the main street, and suddenly I forgot all the questions I had wanted to ask Olaf. I had known him all my life, but in his presence I again felt like a small boy. The village affairs, my love for Heike Brodersen, which wouldn't abate—all that had to seem childish to him. Hemmersmoor and I had nothing to offer him.

"So what's new in the village?" Olaf said.

"Are you staying for good?" I asked instead of answering him.

"Are you trying to get rid of me already?" he asked and laughed.

"No, but . . ." I couldn't go on. "But maybe you need . . ." I stopped again. I decided it was still too early to ask him for work. "Right now everybody in the village is talking about you and your family."

"Is that right?" Olaf seemed curious.

"Anna's . . . Anna . . ." I bit my tongue, and underneath my shock of red hair my face turned red too. I was almost a head shorter than Olaf and didn't have his broad shoulders, but my hands were as big as his. With a broad nail I scratched my cheeks and was happy to feel some stubble. Then I said quickly, "People wonder if Jan will try to get back at you."

Olaf shook his head. "Is he still mad?"

"Once, when he ran into Hilde, he said you wouldn't return, but if you ever should, he'd take care that you left again—on your own feet if you were quick, in a coffin if you weren't. He was drunk though. Your father punched him."

"He didn't tell me," Olaf said.

"Now you know," I said stupidly. "People didn't like it. They said you don't punch a cripple. But if you ask me, Hilde was lucky your dad was there."

Olaf nodded. "What else happened in those seven years?"

"Heidrun Brodersen was arrested for child murder, and Käthe Grimm disappeared."

"Käthe? Crazy Käthe?"

"She went out one night and never returned. She got lost on the bog, for sure."

Olaf cocked his head. "And what have you been up to?"

I shrugged my shoulders, took a deep breath, and said, "I want to buy a moped."

Olaf laughed heartily. "Well, maybe I can help you."

———————

All spring and summer Olaf and Alex worked on the addition to the house, and I helped them in the afternoons after school. On slow days in the pub, even Olaf's father stepped outside, and together we cut wood and hauled and laid bricks and interrupted our work only when Hilde served us a cold supper.

"We missed you," Bernd Frick said one day in June. He wore no shirt, but his muscles were still firm. He wiped his chest with a handkerchief. "Sometimes I wondered whether you would ever return."

"I sent postcards," Olaf said.

"Seven years, thirteen cards. That wasn't much to go on." Bernd wiped his nose and fell silent, but Olaf could see that he wanted to say more and waited patiently.

"You know," his father began, "I always wondered if the stories about the sea, about sailors, were true." He laughed quietly. "You know, a girl in every port, that sort of thing."

Olaf shook his head. "For some, maybe."

"It was a long time. No one would fault you. I for one would not."

"There was hardly enough time to get drunk," Olaf said. "And I had a goal."

"You never wavered? See, I was married for over thirty years, but I faced a few temptations in my time. I've known many who failed." He sighed. "You must have seen many pretty girls in those strange cities. They must have liked a good-looking fellow like you." His words came slowly now, and the smile could no longer hold its place. "Do you have anything you should tell me?"

Olaf swallowed. "Sailors are no angels, and when you're locked up for months, some men go crazy . . ."

"Yeah, some go crazy," Bernd finally said, and laughed and took a long sip from his beer. "I'm glad you finally made it back."

Olaf's first meeting with Jan was a few days later, one evening in front of Frick's Inn. When it got too dark for us to work any longer, Jan suddenly appeared in back of the inn and inspected the half-finished addition. Silently the men looked at each other, and Alex and I took a few steps back; we anticipated a fight. But after another tense moment, Jan shrugged his shoulders, grinned, and said, "Hey, Sailor, how about some booze?"

Olaf invited us all; never had I felt so grown up. At the tables around us sat workers from Brümmer's factory, who laughed boisterously about something old Jens Jensen had just told them. Alex and I drank beer; our clothes were stained and reeked of sweat. We had earned our place among the men, and I earned enough money to have biked to Groß Ostensen two weeks before, to stand in front of the motorcycle dealer's windows and ask for a catalog.

"I'm ugly as hell," Jan said as he took his glass from the bar and sat down at our table. "But I'm not holding a grudge. It's done. Glad you didn't take off my whole arm." The stump was now covered in leather, and Jan said he might be fitted for an artificial hand.

Alex frowned at Jan's words and seemed ready to pounce on him if necessary. He was taller than Olaf and the strongest among us. Yet no fight broke out. Jan and Olaf did not become friends, but they kept the peace. Jan had been allowed to stay at Brümmer's, and even suggested Olaf apply once more. Yet Olaf had talked to the owner of the local repair shop, and since he wasn't getting any younger and had recently lost his best repairman, he'd agreed to sell his business to Olaf once the addition to the inn was finished.

The village made it easy on him—the young girls stopped after school to gawk at the strange drawings on Olaf's arms and back, the neighbors came to lend a hand, and Liese Fitschen often brewed coffee for Olaf or cut him slices from the cakes she baked twice a week.

"Just like in the old days," he said. As a boy he had liked the Fitschens almost better than his own parents, and Liese had given him cookies and candy as often as he came to their door.

"Yes," Liese answered. "You were such a rascal, and now look at you."

Veronika, the youngest of Liese's girls, sometimes stopped at the hedge that separated the two lots, looking up at Olaf without saying a word. Olaf waved each time he spotted the girl, and each time the kid ran off. Olaf laughed and said, "She will still be young enough to play with my own kids."

Veronika's older brothers were more outspoken. Olaf had known them when they hadn't been old enough to attend school, but now he caught them smoking cheap cigars and making passes at girls.

"Did you see the *Klabautermann*?" they wanted to know. "How big was it? Did you see the maelstrom? How did you escape? Did you have many women? How are black women? Yellow ones? Are there really islands where everyone walks about naked?"

The house was finished in July, after school recess had begun, and Liese's children had all day to watch Olaf and bombard him with questions despite their mother's admonitions. Every morning Liese took her youngest to the bakery and let the girl carry the bag with fresh rolls and bread, and shortly afterward the whole family spilled onto the lawn and into the village.

I felt very proud when the topping-out wreath swayed in the light breeze. I stood with a beer in my hand, and my dad patted my back and offered me a cigarette. Bernd Frick seemed satisfied with the work—he poured rye for the neighbors and let himself be photographed with Olaf, Alex, and Hilde. His children had caused him so much pain, but that July night everything seemed changed. Alex and Olaf had come back to Hemmersmoor, and they would finally make him proud.

Only Hilde's face had not brightened when the bottle of rye had been passed around, and she kept to herself all evening. The joyful atmosphere didn't seem to lift her mood, she made a dour face.

"Is it not what you wanted?" Olaf asked.

"It's nice enough," she answered. "I just have to get used to it."

"Do you not love me anymore?" he asked with a smile.

"It's not that." With one of her white, short fingers, she'd traced the grinning demon, drawn in black ink in Shanghai two years before, and refused to hear the story of how and why he'd gotten it. From Alex I knew that Hilde insisted Olaf sleep in his sister's old room, because his tossing and turning kept her awake at night. She showed him bruises from where he'd hit her in his sleep.

"Then what is it?" he asked.

"We were kids when we got married," she said, but before he could hold her back, Hilde rushed off. Olaf saw that I had listened to their conversation and smiled, embarrassed, and shrugged. Even though it was nearly dark, I could see that he was blushing.

Finally the couple moved into the new house and shared the large bed Alex and his father had built together. And to please Hilde, Olaf had a large vanity shipped from Hamburg. Hilde showed it to all the women, and my sister, Birgit, couldn't say enough about the gold-framed mirror. "You can watch yourself combing your hair, doing your makeup, and if I had a husband like Olaf to watch me, I would rub lotion into my skin all day and braid my hair."

"Nonsense," my mother replied. She wasn't impressed by the vanity. "What do you need a golden mirror for? You hair is as coarse as straw, and no matter how much makeup you rub onto your face, you can't hide those freckles."

In late summer Alex applied for a job at the manor, but the only position his former brother-in-law offered him was that of substitute driver. With a special permit, he started the job in September. "If not for my dad, they wouldn't even have hired me as a stable boy," he cursed when I met him one day in full uniform in the village square.

I had bought a moped and was able to drive at night to Groß Ostensen. When we were thirteen, we believed owning a moped was the way into a girl's heart, but the girls in Groß Ostensen didn't care about my moped. As soon as I got off, they could smell Hemmersmoor on me. It was my gait, my face, my way of talking. I carried our village like a yoke.

"Don't waste your time with the pretty ones," Alex advised me. His hair was full of grease, his shined shoes were as large as the boats on the peat bog. "Only the ugly ones put out." That made sense to me, and after two more girls complained that I didn't have any hair on my chest and that my teeth were crooked, I got involved with Linde Janeke. I had kissed her a few times when we were younger, but not once since her accident. None of the girls could stand her, and she never came to any of the dances at Frick's Inn, but after dark we drove out onto the moor. After dark the scars in her face vanished, and her skin glowed very white, and she wrapped herself around me and demanded that I slap her face or hit her with my belt. Only when I obeyed her did she allow me to unbutton my pants.

When we drove through the village at night, we could often see Olaf standing outside the inn or walking the streets. He always seemed to be alone. Hilde was nowhere to be seen, and I couldn't imagine what kept him awake. Perhaps he was missing the sea, I told Linde, but she laughed at me.

"What else could it be?" I asked.

"Silly boy," she said. "If you can't figure it out, I won't tell you."

One night, when I was waiting for her outside the village, Olaf came walking toward me. He was carrying a bundle, and when he recognized me, stepped closer. It was almost midnight, my dad was making his rounds on his bicycle, but here he wouldn't see us. Olaf asked how I was doing and looked at my moped, but my answers were all too short. I was afraid that Linde wouldn't come if she saw him with me, and I hadn't been with her in two days.

"Are you waiting for someone?" he finally asked and smiled.

I nodded, relieved. "What do you have there?" I asked and pointed to his bundle. I didn't want to appear ungrateful.

"Oh," he said. "Knickknacks. I have no use for them anymore." He opened the package, and I recognized the Buddha, the blue scarab, the Statue of Liberty.

"Why do you want to get rid of them?"

He shrugged his shoulders. "Hilde can't stand them. And to me they look unreal now, as though I invented them. Souvenirs are supposed to remind you of things, but here they just look foreign to me. There are no other countries anymore." He was silent for a few moments; then he said, "Here," and put the bundle into my arms. "I wanted to bury them, but maybe you can keep them for me."

"Sure," I said, without knowing what I would do with Olaf's treasures.

Olaf grinned lopsidedly. "Well, I'm gonna leave you now," he said and continued his walk.

"Hey," I shouted. "Thank you."

He turned to look over his shoulder and waved at me.

What happened later at Frick's Inn is often discussed in our village but never questioned. Some speculate that Olaf had fallen ill on one of his long journeys and could be a husband for Hilde no longer. Others suspect that Olaf met too many women in those foreign ports and could never again be happy with just one. A few claim that Olaf had always been a ne'er-do-well and that his father threw him out to prevent further disasters. Nobody tries too hard to find out the truth. The possibilities are too ugly.

That night I waited until Linde arrived, and together we drove to an old barn near Brümmer's factory. "I'm not made from sugar," she soon complained. I tore open her shirt and squeezed her breasts, which were as small as macaroons, their tips as dark as chocolate. Her first blow hit my right ear, and for seconds I could hear only a loud ringing noise. I tried to grip her arms, but her forehead hit my mouth, and I tasted blood and she laughed at me. "You're like a drizzle—I don't get wet." Then she hit my shin, stomped with one of her heels onto my toes. This time I punched her in the face, right on the chin. I hit her harder and she fell quiet, froze. I tore her panties, slapped her thighs and her face. She trembled without making a sound, waited for my blows, and I obeyed. Finally she turned around, propped herself up on the seat of the moped and stuck her ass out for me. But the ground was sandy, and the kickstand gave way, and Linde and the moped fell down.

I pulled her up, pushed her aside, and inspected my moped. Was something bent, had Linde stepped on the spokes? I wiped off the handlebars with her panties, and everything still seemed intact. To be sure, I started the moped, but when the engine roared to life, I noticed that Linde was no longer inside the barn. I called her name, but she didn't answer. In my ears I could still hear her laughter, her sneer. I didn't go to the trouble of looking for her.

Shortly after handing me his bundle, Olaf returned home. At least that's what Alex has told me. The whole affair disgusted him, he said, but he seemed hell-bent on telling me his story. And when I later jumped up and said he better shut his mouth, he insisted I hear him out.

He had arrived home from work in the evening, and was sitting at the bar, when Olaf entered the pub and joined him. The brothers didn't say a word to each other, but shortly after his arrival, Olaf felt a hand on his shoulder.

"Shouldn't you be at home with your wife?" It was Jan,

smiling, holding a glass of beer in his right hand and touching Olaf with his new prosthetic left. Olaf disregarded the fact that Jan was not his friend. Perhaps his tongue wanted to get rid of the words that clogged his throat and mouth. "That's just it," he exclaimed. "Ever since I've come back, she treats me like a stranger."

Alex got up to pour the men another shot of rye. Jan sat down next to Olaf, slumping over his glass of beer, looking up at the young sailor with sympathy. "You were gone for many years, a long time even for a godforsaken village like ours. You were gone more years than you were ever together."

"Yet it won't get any better," Olaf said. "I tried, and yet she resists me."

"It still might," Jan said. "It still might. My wife and I," he raised his new hand into the air and waved it in front of Olaf's face, "we've had our ups and downs. When we're alone, she kills all the lights so she doesn't have to see who's touching her."

"But you . . . ," Olaf said and immediately stopped himself.

"I am crippled, sure."

"I'm sorry, Jan," Olaf said. "I really am."

Jan continued without listening to Olaf's apologies. His voice became quieter and sweeter still. "But there are far more ugly things than my hand."

"What are you saying?" Olaf said, and Alex could see his brother's face flush and his shoulders tighten.

"You were gone for a long time, a long time for a young girl. People doubted you'd be back. She is beautiful."

"You're drunk," Olaf said. "I won't stand for your talk."

"Oh you want to punch me like your old man did? First you cripple me and then you hit me? But you're right," he said and got up from his stool, smiling once more, his voice still as quiet and pleasant as before. "I'm drunk." He left Olaf to rejoin the small group of workers from Brümmer's. But before he did, he turned to Olaf once more. "All the bad things I could wish on you, you've already done to yourself. Go home, Sailor. Tell Liese Fitschen her Veronika looks just as cute as her mother."

That night Olaf did not go to sleep. Alex kept him company long after the inn had closed. The two brothers were alone and drank; Olaf did not dare enter his wife's bedroom.

In the early morning, they were already standing outside the Fitschens' gate, waiting for Liese and her little girl to appear. Alex has assured me that he tried to dissuade his brother from doing so, but he wouldn't listen. When Liese and Veronika finally stepped out onto the street and greeted their neighbors, they didn't receive an answer. Instead Olaf picked up the child and stared at her face.

"What are you doing?" Liese asked with suspicion in her voice, but Alex motioned for her to keep quiet.

"She looks nothing like you," Olaf said.

"Let go of her," Liese demanded. "She's mine."

The girl started to cry. She had Hilde's mouth, her round cheeks. She even had the same large blue eyes.

"It can't be," Olaf said and turned to his brother. But Alex nodded without a word. The likeness couldn't be denied.

"You can't take her," Liese said and started to cry herself. "She's mine."

"When was she born? I'll strangle her if you don't answer me." Olaf took hold of the girl's soft braids.

"Four years ago, in March, four years. She's mine, she's mine I swear. I swear to you, Olaf, she's mine."

"You're lying," Olaf said, but finally he set down the girl, whose face was wide with fear. "She's her daughter, Hilde's girl. Jan knows the truth. Probably the whole village knows you're lying to me."

When the two brothers returned home, Hilde stood in the living room and behind her appeared Bernd Frick. The lines in the old man's face appeared even deeper than usual. "I heard the ruckus outside," Hilde said. "I was worried. What did you want from Liese?"

"The girl is your daughter," Olaf said, his words barely slipping past his tongue. "Who is the father?"

"Nonsense," Bernd Frick said. "What an idea."

"Why do you deny it? She looks like Hilde. Why did you give her away? Who is the father? Who?"

For a long time nobody spoke. Hilde stood with her gaze directed toward the floor and her bare feet. Finally Olaf's father said, "She thought you were dead."

"And you covered it up for her. Took her to Liese." Olaf took a few steps forward and struck his father with his fists. The older man's head flew back and then his knees buckled; he slumped to the floor.

With a shriek, Hilde flew toward Bernd, covering his head with her hair. She held him tight, rocking him, stroking his cheeks. "Yes," she said to Olaf, "we both hoped you'd never come back."

When asked what had happened to Olaf Frick, people in Hemmersmoor shrugged. "The call of the sea," the baker volunteered. "All these years in those godless countries, they leave a mark on you."

The mailman wouldn't say; he never received another post-card from Shanghai or Macao. Soon enough, the village girls redirected their attention to Rutger von Kamphoff, who looked even more suave now that he was wearing black. He was once more available, and every young woman wanted to know how in the world she could get invited to the manor.

Jan Hussel, when asked, stroked the black fingers of his prosthetic hand. "Stupid affair," he said and shook his head. "He could have made good after all." He seemed genuinely distressed and said that he regretted not having had the opportunity to talk to Olaf one last time.

Listening to Jan's answer, Alex shrugged. He had made me swear not to betray his secret; he had to protect the family's reputation as well as its business. He wouldn't always be the von Kamphoffs' driver. Whenever the people in the village mentioned Olaf, he shook his head. "Not enough life around here."

Anke

Through my scholarship, which I started in the fall, I stayed in contact with the Big House, and sometimes I received an invitation to one of the dinner parties there. My mother was beside herself with joy, and when the black Mercedes stopped in front of our house, she would have liked to gather the whole neighborhood to watch me get into the car. "Rutger has an eye on you," she reassured me each and every day. "Keep in close touch with him." She didn't know just how well I followed her advice. I kept quiet about the meetings Rutger arranged for us from time to time, and which he kept secret from his family. He still wore black.

One day in the spring, just before Easter, I came home to find the house empty. My mother had pushed my lunch into the oven, and in her note, which I found on the kitchen table, she wrote that she would spend the afternoon in Groß Ostensen. My dad was working on the fields with my brothers and wouldn't be home before dinner.

I sighed in relief. The more time I spent at the Big House, the smaller my own home seemed to become. I hated the smells that wafted from our kitchen through the whole house, and I couldn't watch my father eat anymore. It was horrible how noisily he slurped his soup; after every bite of meat he scratched between his teeth with his fingernails. My brothers chewed with their mouths open while continuing their conversations. I was only too happy not to find any of them at home. I'd be able to prepare for my rendezvous with Rutger undisturbed. The chauffeur would pick me up at four o'clock.

Rutger's marriage with Anna Frick had scandalized his family, and only Frick's money had finally convinced Bruno von Kamphoff and his wife to relent. Anna had been one of us, a village beauty with rosy cheeks and without manners. I knew what happened when girls like us got mixed up with people like the von Kamphoffs. And even though I sensed that Rutger meant well, I had not entirely given in to his greed. My dad wasn't as rich as Frick. I had only my young skin and my brown hair. Nobody had touched me yet.

This is what I thought while washing myself and putting on a new dress, one that Rutger hadn't yet seen dozens of times. I brushed my hair and pushed away pictures of my friend Linde. How much better was I prepared to take advantage of the opportunity I was given. She would only have squandered it. And, anyway, her face was disfigured—she had even less to offer the future heir of the Big House.

Around three o'clock I heard a car in front of the house, and with surprise I saw that it was really the von Kamphoffs' black Mercedes. The driver got out, walked slowly toward our door. Had he been given the wrong time?

With hair loose and without any makeup, I ran down the stairs and opened the door. How big was my surprise when I found not the elegant young man I was used to but Alex Frick taking off his black cap and grinning at me. "Anke?" he said. "The car is ready."

"You?" I said. I couldn't explain Alex's appearance. "What is this?" I knew that Frick's younger son had returned to Hemmersmoor, but I hadn't seen much of him in the village. My parents had not frequented Frick's Inn since Broder's death; Alex's light punishment, they said, had been bought from the authorities. Three years for a son. What kind of justice was that?

"Indeed," Alex said. "I'm the new chauffeur. Can I come in?"

"The chauffeur?" I asked.

"Oh, are you already one of them?"

"You are too early," I said and heard how stupid this sounded. "That's not what I meant. You shouldn't be here. If my mother comes home . . ."

"Not before dinnertime."

"You don't know that."

"And your father is working in the fields. You're all dolled up." Alex inspected me from top to bottom. He couldn't have been more than eighteen years old, but he had grown a lot and was as heavy and slow moving as a much older man. He looked funny in his uniform, funny and somehow adorable, like a circus bear. He had the lazy movements of a man who knows he can punch holes into a wall.

Alex crossed the doorstep without my invitation. I had to move to avoid him. "Go, get yourself ready," he said. "I'll wait down here."

"If my parents find out . . . ," I said.

"I know what I did. But I've lost a sister." Alex looked around our entrance hall. "I know how it feels."

"I had nothing to do with that," I said angrily.

"I didn't say you did." He smiled. "But it looks as if you might take her place. Rutger was very particular when he gave me instructions."

I felt myself blushing. Had Rutger talked about me with Alex? I was flattered to hear that Rutger did indeed have plans for me, but how could he talk about them with his driver? What was he thinking, sending Alex to our house? Didn't he know what had happened?

"Perhaps he'll fire me if you ask him real nicely." Alex's smile grew wider, until I couldn't look him in the eyes anymore. "I've paid the price, Anke," he added. "I don't expect your parents to like me, but what happened was nothing but a stupid prank. I was a boy. I didn't mean to kill your brother."

Speechless, I stood in the hall; I was still holding my brush in my left hand.

"I'll wait in the car," Alex finally said. "Ms. Hoffmann." He nodded and adjusted his cap.

I was utterly confused. I wanted to tell my mom about what had just happened, wanted to run into the fields to search for my father. I wanted to meet Rutger. Finally I ran up the stairs to my room and put on makeup. I wanted to find good reasons for Alex's appearance, and I found them all too quickly: he was Anna's brother, he needed work, and at the Big House he was still near his father, without having to show his face in Hemmersmoor much. Besides, Rutger would never have heard of my brother's death—our lives weren't part of the von Kamp-hoffs' conversations.

Twenty minutes after he'd arrived, Alex opened the car door for me, closed it carefully, and soon we had left the village behind us. The radio was playing with the volume turned low. A singer from Hamburg could be heard, yearning for white sails, sailors, and foreign lands. The skies hung low over the fields, rolled out like down comforters. It was one of those days that promised warmth and sun but still held back both. Light green showed on the bushes along the road; everything looked clean and polished. I was wearing only a light cardigan over my dress and goose bumps spread on my arms. Perhaps it would rain later on.

He didn't ask once. He rolled down the window, and even though it messed up my hair, so that I had to move away, he kept it open. Halfway to the manor, close to an old barn that hadn't been used since a fire had nearly destroyed it, Alex braked and let the car slowly roll ahead. I watched the blackened roof of the barn and the large holes in its walls.

"One day I'll take over my father's inn," he said.

"Yes," I said.

"Can I help you with something? I still have to drive the old man to a show in Bremen tonight. I don't have much time."

I shook my head as an answer to his peculiar question. "I don't need anything."

"I have some coffee with me." He reached under his seat and a moment later came up with an orange thermos. "It's only lukewarm."

"No thanks," I said cautiously.

"Not very hot." Alex stopped the car. He unscrewed the top of the thermos and poured himself some coffee. "It doesn't matter to me that it's lukewarm. The body absorbs lukewarm liquids better."

"Oh," I said.

"Read it somewhere."

"Fine," I said.

Alex drank the black coffee and then switched off the engine. He opened his door and inhaled deeply. "The air gives me the hiccups," he said, and belched into his hand and laughed. Then he got out, put his cup on the roof of the car, and stretched.

"We should continue," I said. "Rutger is waiting."

"Sure," Alex said. "Sure thing." Then he opened the left passenger door and sat down next to me.

"We'll be late," I said.

"Maybe." Alex stretched out his hand and touched my breast.

"Hey." I forced myself to laugh; it could only be a stupid joke.

"Hey," he echoed and put his other hand on my hip. His hands were enormous, his fingers thick and short. Short hairs sprouted on them.

I scooted all the way to the right, and he followed me. I grabbed the door handle and pulled, but Alex's left hand closed around my arm and he simply shook his head. Then his hand cupped my other breast.

I could have screamed, I could have tried to push open the car door and run away, but I didn't want him to hit me. "Rutger will . . . ," I said and couldn't finish the sentence.

Alex nodded. "You look funny," he then said.

The soft afternoon light filled the car, and when he pressed me down onto the backseat, for one short moment I could see the pale sun behind a thin layer of clouds. Then Alex's face appeared above me. All this happened slowly; he didn't rush, didn't show any haste. He sat on top of me, unbuttoned his jacket and threw it onto the front seat. Then he loosened his tie and pulled it over his head. He unbuttoned his shirt and let it drop onto the seat next to my face. Finally Alex raised himself as much as he could and opened his pants.

"You know," he said, "my brother had all these funny drawings on his skin."

I nodded. I hadn't seen them myself, but my friends had told me about Olaf's tattoos.

"Some of the boys in that institution had them too." He paused for a moment. "I don't think I could carry around the same symbol or picture for the rest of my life. Or a name." He seemed to think about this diligently, as though he wanted to make sure he got the words right. "'Anke,' for example. I mean, if you don't like that girl anymore, it's still there, and you're constantly reminded of her."

My voice was very low and hoarse. It seemed important to answer him. "Maybe a shape, a simple one. Maybe a triangle, a circle, or a square."

Alex laughed—he seemed to be genuinely amused. "A square. Simple," he repeated and grinned.

"Yeah, a black square. Doesn't have to mean anything. Just a square."

"'Hey, what's that mean?' 'Why, I love squares,'" he said, and we both laughed. My voice shrilled in my ears.

"Yeah, a square," I said.

Alex was quiet for a while, sat in his underwear next to me in the backseat. "I'd like to see somebody tattoo his body onto his body."

"What do you mean?" I asked. His hands had forgotten about me. Say something, Anke, I told myself, keep it up. Just say something, just talk and occupy him. Occupy him.

"The shape of his body tattooed onto his skin, just a bit smaller, so it fits. His fingers drawn onto his fingers, his arms onto his arms. Well, the face would be difficult."

I tried to smile. "The eyes, yeah. The nose—you could do that."

"And one thing would be missing. You know, he'd have the whole body tattooed on his body, but one hand would be missing, or a calf. And everybody would look at the missing limb, because it's just missing."

"That would be strange," I said. "Would you tattoo the skeleton onto the skin as well?"

"Maybe," he said absentmindedly, but I could hear that he hadn't given it a thought. "There would be two people, only one would be incomplete." With those words he moved a little away from me, lifted up the hem of my dress and pulled down my panties. The radio was still playing, the singer had a famously clear voice, and she sang about islands in the sea and deadly typhoons. Alex climbed out of the car and turned his back on me. He dropped his pants to the ground. His back had two or three red spots but was otherwise completely white. He focused entirely on untying his shoe laces and seemed to forget about me. I listened to the music, made plans to jump out of the car and escape Alex, whose pants still hung around his ankles. I had time. I was fast. I would succeed. But Alex's presence, his massive white back, rendered all plans incomprehensible, and when he stepped out of his shoes, I hadn't even tried to run. I was just lying in the backseat, waiting until he was ready for me.

Alex turned, climbed into the car, lay down heavily on my chest and forced himself into me. He didn't face me but seemed to look out the rear window. He didn't try to kiss me.

When he was done, he kept lying on top of me. Behind me I could see a narrow strip of sky; in front of me loomed Alex's head with its greased hair. The singer received much applause for her ballad about a lonely sailor, and then launched into a song about the *Klabautermann.* The audience joined in for the chorus.

I had imagined that Alex would get up immediately and start to dress. I had thought that he would hit me, that I might avoid being hit if I lay completely still. I had thought that as soon as he was done he would get behind the wheel once more. But he only sat up, dangled his legs, put his head out the door, and stared into the sky. The audience grew louder and louder and clapped in rhythm with the song about the *Klabau-termann,* and in that moment, when I realized that I had no idea what Alex wanted from me and what he had planned, I knew I would lose my sanity. I had been paralyzed with fear, but I had been proud of myself that I hadn't screamed and kicked, that I hadn't given him a reason to beat me. Now, however, he sat at my feet, one hand on my leg, and leaned back in the seat. I'm not sure if he fell asleep, I think he wasn't asleep, but he sat next to me and put his hand between my legs and I could feel how warm his hand was. Alex breathed steadily, sat next to me in the backseat, and closed his eyes.

In that moment I left my body, and I'm not sure I ever

returned. The program ended and a new one began; this one an opera, and all the members of the audience coughed and then fell quiet, and then the instruments started up. Alex and I lay on the backseat, and it started to rain. I could hear the drops fall onto the roof. And I didn't fear anything as much as I feared the music, the bright brass section, the violins, the singers' laughing voices.

I wished to get up and switch off the radio, but I didn't want to alarm Alex. I could smell him now, his sweat had mixed with his aftershave. It was a terrible stench. Alex's cheeks were soft, and he had a snub nose with large pores, and fleshy lips. His ears were small and fat.

Finally he sighed, got to his feet, and hummed along with the music. He looked over his shoulder at me, and only then did I realize how rigidly I lay in the backseat. I was a wooden puppet he had thrown in back.

Slowly, Alex pulled up his pants. He was looking for his shirt; his hair stood straight up on top, like the comb of a rooster. And as if he had noticed himself, he smoothed it with both hands. Then he nodded his head, perhaps looking to find the appropriate words, but instead he began to whistle—with too much air to produce a clear tone.

He buttoned his shirt, fastened his tie, and went to the hood of the car. I was still in the backseat, and I was overcome with panic as if I only now fully realized what had happened. But I still could not stir—the slightest movement would break me in half.

"Is my tie straight?" Alex asked. His head appeared again in the door.

I shook my head. Carefully, inch by inch, I pulled down my dress. He did not seem to notice.

"Could you . . . ?" he asked.

I sat up, and it started dripping out of me. I stifled a scream. Carefully, I climbed out of the car and pulled at Alex's tie.

"Thank you." He turned around, moved his shoulders in circles, turned and twisted his neck like a boxer testing if everything felt right. Then he lit a cigarette. There was no traffic on the road to the Big House, not even a bicycle or a horse-drawn cart. It was still raining, but it did not seem to bother Alex. "As a boy I wanted to open your blouse," he said, shaking his head. "Are you ready?" He was in no hurry.

And I realized that haste was not necessary. Not for Alex, not even for me. There was nothing I could escape from. I could still hear the music coming from inside the car, a passionate aria, a female and a male voice wrapping themselves around each other, and although I could think of nothing but this music, I knew that Alex was not afraid, and that I would never tell Rutger anything about this trip or the next. If I ever opened my mouth, Alex would be dismissed from the estate, perhaps even arrested. And Rutger? What would he do after he was finished with his driver? What words would he use to get rid of me?

With my embroidered handkerchief I wiped the backseat before getting back into the car. The rain hadn't cooled the air, it was still soft, and Alex didn't close the window when he got behind the wheel.

I could have told on Rutger, but I never did, not that afternoon and not later. My goal to live at his side demanded that I keep my mouth shut, and it was important that Alex keep quiet too. After a short while, that silence gave me the feeling that I was the one who had committed a crime. I had not been raped; I had done it to another.

Sometimes, when the black car appeared at our front door, I felt weak and humiliated, but after a few weeks it seemed to me that Alex and I were allies. My disgust subsided, and from then on Alex and his car seemed to give me strength. His presence was preparing me for my new life, his touch was only a prelude to Rutger's greed. In Alex's car I was his accomplice. It couldn't be otherwise.

That afternoon Alex looked once more in the rearview mirror, made sure everything was in order, and started the engine. The gravel crunched under our tires as we drove away from the old barn. Over the music he said, "Next time you can show a little more feeling."

Christian

On a small chest of drawers in our living room stood the photographs of my family. Nicole and Ingrid as toddlers in our garden, both of them wearing white dresses. Nicole at her confirmation in front of the church. My parents' wedding picture, taken in Frick's Inn. My grandmother had kept her eyes closed, and the ring bearer's face was blurry because he hadn't sat still. Not a single photo had me in it. My mother had banned me from the family even while I was still living in her house.

One photo of my dad was of special interest to me in those days. It showed him as a young man wearing a leather jacket over his white uniform. Next to him stood the baker, whose right hand rested on my father's shoulder, and who also laughed at the camera. Both men wore hats with stiff black bills, almost like the police, and they stood in front of their delivery vans, which were parked next to each other. In the background several men unloaded milk and large crates full of bread. They wore uniforms and wore their hair as short as soldiers.

My mother hadn't removed a single picture of my late father, but it was this one I looked at almost daily. I was in love with

Sylvia Meier, the baker's daughter, and this picture seemed to connect our families. It was a source of pleasure and a certain discomfort to see the two men smiling at me together. It seemed as though my father had meddled with my life and love even before I was born. At times when I looked at Sylvia's face and ran my fingers over her nose and cheeks, it was as though my dad were leading my hand and Sylvia were looking not at me but him.

When my mother caught me one morning with that photo in my hands, she hit my face repeatedly. My nose started to bleed, and one of her rings cut my forehead. The teacher often admonished me not to brawl—I looked all raw, he said. My white, almost translucent skin was a map of my mother's wrath.

At night I left the house to meet Sylvia at our usual spot on the banks of the Droste. Sylvia had kissed many boys, and she had already done it with several of them. She was experienced. I was barely her height, but she said I was special and had not once missed an appointed meeting. She felt the small hills of my scars, kissed my burns, my bruises, and licked them. In the dark she ran her tongue over every bump of my skin, and since spring was near, we were half-naked and panting. Sylvia unbuttoned my pants and pulled down my underwear. She showed me how to unclasp her bra, asked if I weren't curious to see how she looked without her pantyhose.

Often our encounters lasted several hours, but that night Sylvia soon told me to put my clothes back on, and then walked away from the river.

"Where are we going?" I asked.

She laughed, her legs naked and stockings stuffed into

one of her coat pockets. We strode past the last houses of Hemmersmoor, across barren fields. The night was damp, thousands of fine drops clung to our bodies. But we were warm.

"Are we meeting someone?" I asked.

Sylvia kissed me, pulling my hand down to touch her. "Be quiet, Christian," she whispered.

I trusted her, and yet I grew concerned as we made our way farther and farther out onto the moor. After a while the rows of drying peat bricks grew scarce, and only hard grasses covered the soil. Clouds as large as continents blew over our heads. Hemmersmoor had long since disappeared behind us.

After half an hour she finally slowed. In front of us scraggly trees rose and waved their branches, and after a few more steps, we came to a gate, rusty barbed wire curling at our feet.

"You're not scared, are you?" Sylvia scaled the iron gate, her legs shining even in the dark.

I followed her. "What is this?" I asked. "Do they have dogs?"

Sylvia shushed me. "Don't be afraid. No one's here."

We were walking along a narrow paved road, and soon we reached a low barrack. Its door was locked, but Sylvia opened a window on the far side of the building, and we climbed inside. She flicked a switch, and we stood among thirty bunk beds, their mattresses bare, some stained. The room smelled of dust, yet the overall effect was one of cleanliness.

Sylvia's blond hair was glittering with moisture under the single bare bulb that dangled from the ceiling. Her cheeks were red.

"Who lives here?"

"No one," she said, and kicked off her shoes.

Three weeks later she said she'd fallen in love with someone else, a twenty-year-old soccer player, and that we couldn't see each other anymore.

I couldn't sleep, and I couldn't tell anyone. My mother was not allowed to know; my sister Nicole had no time for "that monster." She had a little baby to take care of and couldn't be bothered. Whatever I confessed to her would go straight to my mother.

Images of Sylvia doing what we had done with a new boy, an older boy, kept me sobbing at night. But even worse was when, after two days of mourning, I plunged into such hopelessness that I didn't even have the strength to conjure up any haunting images. My world turned black.

After a week I decided to go to the place Sylvia had shown me. Just the thought of returning to that barrack revived my pain, and I felt grateful for it. I would spy on her, I decided. I would watch Sylvia with her new lover. I'd be so close to her, so close.

My task turned out to be more difficult than I had imagined. A walk after school one May afternoon proved futile. The daylight barricaded my way; after an hour of crisscrossing the moor, I stood in ankle-deep mud, with nothing in sight. My memory was useless.

During supper, I tried to steer my family's conversation toward the subject of a gated area, an empty barrack somewhere north of our village. Maybe my mother or sister knew of that place.

"A barrack?" Nicole asked. Her son had fed and was sleeping in her lap; she never let me come close to him.

"Thomas said, in school, that he'd seen one outside the

village. He said there was a gate." I stared at my salami sandwich, unable to meet her eyes.

"Maybe he's seen one of the vacation homes around here," Mother said. My dad's chair at the table was not to be touched or moved, and every evening she put out a plate for him.

"Probably just a barn," my sister replied. "Thomas isn't all that bright. Neither are his parents."

I tried again to reach that gate after nightfall. How strange that once it had grown dark, my feet knew just where to go and my eyes followed my memories. Sylvia, of course, was not with me, but I hoped to see her at the barrack.

I scaled the fence once more, found the barrack dark and locked. I listened for sounds from inside but heard nothing. Instead of climbing through a window, I headed down the paved road.

After only fifty yards, another barrack appeared to my right, then another. A fourth one, and the road was still leading ahead. To my left a large barnlike structure shot up, and through an unlocked gate, which I slid open, I entered. It was darker than night inside, but after a few moments, I made out large machines, squatting like reptiles. Tiny feet scurried over the floor, glass crunched under my shoes. My whistling came echoing back at me, and I hurried outside.

I was still following the road when I came to a railroad crossing. Hemmersmoor's only track ended at Brümmer's factory—did this track extend to Brümmer's? Or was it unconnected to the appearance of the small steam engine we boys had admired for so long?

Walking from one end of Hemmersmoor to the other took me twenty minutes. I had walked twenty minutes on the winding road when I came to a barrack whose front door was busted. On entering I found that, just like in the first building, the light was still working. In the back, I stepped into an enormous kitchen with several stationary frying pans, gas burners as big as the stove surface at my own home, and pots into which I still would have fit entirely. Enormous cooking spoons and whisks lay strewn on the floor, like the toys of some ancient race of giants.

A large hall with wooden floors and long wooden tables lay adjacent to this kitchen, and while some of the chairs had been broken, this hall still seemed to wait for hundreds of hungry eaters. Who had been living here? I didn't dare switch off the light.

The road ended, and a small path continued on. By the time I found myself walking among bushes and small trees, I had given up thoughts of Sylvia and her new boyfriend. I had discovered a village larger than my own, but with no streetlights and no one around. It lay so close to Hemmersmoor, and yet the place didn't seem to know that. I saw no cars, no bicycles or mopeds. I had often been out and about at night, meeting Sylvia in one dark corner of Hemmersmoor or another. Even if all lights were extinguished by the time we held each other, there was a certain thickness we could feel on our skin, people in their beds not far away dreaming bad dreams, their stomachs churning. I could feel their presence just like I felt the night on my skin when Sylvia pulled open my shirt. Here the air felt empty. Only echoes of the people who had once lived here remained.

The dirt path ended in front of a field much larger than the soccer field behind our school and framed by high hedges. If it was at all possible, this place seemed quieter even than the rest of the dark village. Stone slabs on the ground led me across the field to the far end of it. Wreaths lay rotting around a monument. It was too dark to read the inscription, but when I stooped to look at one of the wreaths, I could decipher a word on one of the smudged bows. "Souvenir." I was standing in a cemetery. The cemetery of this town I knew nothing about. Who had left the wreaths? Where had they gone?

On my way back, I ran, not out of fear, but a sense of wonder. I sped along the narrow road, past the barracks, making sure everything I had discovered was still there. I shook my head in laughter and disbelief. How was it possible that a whole village could be so close to my own and yet unknown? I felt like an explorer, having found the last white spot on the map. Better still, I had accessed it, I believed, through a secret door. I had found a magic opening in the confines of my petty life and slipped into a parallel Hemmersmoor. I felt powerful that night, as though I had made everyone in my village disappear. The master of a world only I could see and enter.

I was wrong, of course. It dawned on me when I saw a flag fluttering from one of the schoolboys' bikes. It was attached to a rod the boy had wired to the frame, so it would stick out behind his seat. On this little flag, I could read "enir," and I instantly knew where he had found his treasure. That same afternoon, feeling that my mysterious kingdom had been invaded, I followed the railroad track from Brümmer's factory north, and after half an hour I ended up in my ghost town. Everyone had known about it, long before Sylvia had led me there. My face turned crimson, even though no one was around.

When Sylvia and I got back together, for a few short weeks in the summer, we did it in the cemetery, and only later noticed that the monument had been smeared with blood. Entrails, pigs' hooves, and pigs' heads hung from the stone. Sylvia couldn't find her panties.

Broken windows, graffiti, overturned beds—in the next two years I noticed how much traffic my ghost town attracted. I never met anyone else there, and yet I was never alone. Then the town was turned into a camp for youths from that other Germany. I had heard stories about it, had seen it on maps. Our Germany was depicted in pink, theirs in red.

They appeared in small groups in Hemmersmoor, hanging out in front of Frick's and getting in fights with the apprentices of Brümmer's factory. Alex had been released from juvenile prison after three years, and when he didn't work as the von Kamphoffs' driver, he got involved in the fights as well. Nobody wanted the strangers, not even Mr. Meier, the baker, seemed happy about delivering hundreds of rolls every morning to the other village.

This was my last year of school, and with some luck, I would graduate. What would happen afterward I couldn't say. Martin made plans to attend university in Hamburg. Alex would start managing Frick's Inn. Rumors made the rounds, ugly rumors that Hilde had given birth to a bastard child, and that the old owner was paying large sums of money to suppress the truth. But the rumors didn't seem to bother the Fricks; their inn was always crowded. Rumors proved good business.

I was standing in our village square one morning when Mr. Meier returned from one of his deliveries to the camp and started unloading the empty crates with a sour face. When he noticed my presence, he beckoned to me to come closer. I didn't know whether he knew that Sylvia had slept with me, and I approached his van with hesitation. Yet the baker only asked if I wanted to earn some fresh rolls, and I helped him carry the crates into the bakery. "Say hello to your mother," he said when we were done and entering the store. Several women were standing in front of the counter and talking to Mrs. Meier. He patted my back and told his wife to bring me a bag of rolls.

And it was in this moment, when rouged and brightly smiling Mrs. Meier was handing me the rolls and Mr. Meier was putting his hand once more on my shoulder, that I remembered the photograph of my dad and knew at once where it had been taken. I tore the bag from the baker's wife's hands and ran home.

It was still early. My sister hadn't taken her place on the kitchen bench yet. Her son's voice wasn't yet filling the room. I ran into the living room and grabbed the photo in which my father and the baker laughed at the camera. Only one man in the background was wearing a real uniform, a peaked cap and a rifle. The other men, whom I had taken for soldiers all these years, were wearing gray clothes, their heads had been shaved. And the building in front of which the two vans were parked I had entered myself not long ago—with awe I had picked up the large spoons and ladles.

Shame and humiliation painted my face red. Not only had I been dead last to discover this building and the village in which it stood, but also my father had entered it long before me. Before Sylvia had led me to the barracks, and the people from this other Germany came to live there, my father and the baker had delivered milk and bread to this village. Soldiers had policed the people living there.

That night I ran to Sylvia. She said she had no time for me—she had to meet her new boyfriend. She unbuttoned my shirt and searched my skin for scratches and burn marks. Her hair hadn't been combed, and she smelled of summer and sweat. The hairs in her armpits were wet and I rubbed my face in them.

"I will leave Hemmersmoor soon," I said, and tried to get used to the sound of these words. "You want to come?" I wanted to leave, but whenever I thought about what lay behind our village, I saw only half-dreamed thoughts and glittering landscapes without contours or colors. And whenever I managed to visualize the streets of Hamburg or some other big city, I was nowhere to be seen. However beautiful the picture was, I remained invisible.

"Not really," Sylvia said. She put my dick inside her and sighed as though she had tasted a particularly nice piece of cake.

I stayed in Hemmersmoor the next day and the next week. My packed suitcase stayed under my bed. And before it was winter, the youths from the East were gone; the barracks hadn't been built for them anyway.

Nobody shed a tear for the youths, and what had happened to the people who had lived in the camp before them, nobody was interested in either. Despite the photo in my living room, despite the vans that had delivered groceries to this other village on a daily basis, and despite the railroad track that led right through it, nobody in Hemmersmoor could say who the people in the camp had been. Nobody remembered the ones who had lived there, slept in the barracks, and died. There had never been such people.

Epilogue

The night after the funeral, when I stop by the inn for a glass of beer, Hilde, Alex's wife, is behind the bar and nods at me. She is plump and her hair is cut short and dyed a shade of red, with blond highlights running through it. Hardly anyone remembers that she was once married to Alex's brother, Olaf. Hilde's second marriage has not produced any children, and Alex worries about the future. He complains about heartburn. Who will inherit the inn and the new hotel and riding stables?

Autographed photos of regional celebrities hang behind the bar. They are made out to Alex, praising his food and his liquor. A singer in a white suit and with curly hair, who once crooned about warm nights in Naples and the starry skies above Capri, smiles down at me; a newscaster looks serious in black and white, and the mayor of Bremen watches me from behind his dark glasses and bares his teeth.

Yet Martin has spurned Alex's invitation and hasn't come. From time to time, Alex buys pricey oil paintings from his school friend, pictures of local landscapes with threatening clouds and blooming moorlands. In them the skies take up nearly the whole canvas and maim houses and farms. Alex claims that Martin's store wouldn't survive without his patronage. He's told me that he'll take care of his friend's family should something tragic happen to Martin. He has created trust funds for Martin and Veronika's children, but he has never spoken to them. Martin makes sure that Alex sees them only from afar.

Linde has not come to Frick's Inn either. Maybe she has found peace; maybe she's finally even with Anke. Or maybe she's still waiting for her scholarship, still waiting for the black Mercedes to slowly drive into the village and pull up in front of her ramshackle house, and for Anke to get out of the car, open the gate to the garden, and knock on the door. But maybe she hates Alex even more and can't forgive him for what he once did to her hated friend.

I look around and overhear a young man talk with contempt about the legends of giants and wizards. "What a dreadful landscape," he says to his female companion. He has pushed his sunglasses up into his hair, even though it's dark outside and pouring relentlessly. "It's flat, swampy, and always gray. And look at the people." He doesn't lower his voice as he continues his tirade. "Incest. Narrow shoulders, wide hips, and large feet. Everybody is everybody else's cousin. And they still believe in ghosts."

"I've seen the will-o'-the-wisps with my own eyes." I should keep my mouth shut, but the funeral feels like a giant rock in my stomach. One fight is as good as the next.

The young man turns around to face me. "Really?" he says and laughs tauntingly. "How much have you had to drink, old man?"

I glare at him, and the girl at his side talks to him in a whisper. I lift my glass and say, "Sometimes you can still see them today."

The young man laughs too loudly. "Boo," he says. "How terrifying."

Yet at that moment Alex appears behind the bar. "Shut up," he bellows at the young man. "If you don't like it here, then piss off."

Then he takes a construction blueprint from behind the bar and spreads it in front of me. "I'll tear down the old stables, build better and bigger ones." He points with a thick finger to a point on the paper. "The house is rotted through. The rats have pissed and shit on every floor and every beam. But the foundation is still solid. We'll rebuild the house just as it was. I retrieved the old blueprints. Outside everything will look like in the old days, only on the inside we'll modernize. Everything will be top notch. Twenty hotel rooms, all of them with a good-sized bath, a few with Jacuzzis. The rooms will be made to feel authentic. All the materials will be first class." He continues talking this way, but he suddenly seems to have lost interest. He casts down his gaze, then looks at me questioningly. "That Linde—she's one crazy old hag, isn't she? 'You killed her.'" He rubs his cheek—he's still feeling her hand slap him. His eyes are waiting for an answer, and I don't provide him with one. "Well," he says and grunts. "It wasn't my fault the two of them didn't get along." He looks as though he's been badly wronged. "It's the truth."

Hilde joins us later. She will run the hotel, she says. Alex will have to look for someone new to help out at the inn. "Not too young, not too plump," she adds with a smile, and strokes her husband's cheek. Her lips open in a kiss. Alex puts his arm around her shoulder. "She worries about my heart," he says. "When God takes away our ability, why doesn't he also take our desire with it?" His teeth are full of gold.

Time is of no importance. Despite the rain, I don't walk straight home. Only at night, when the noise of the cars abates and the streets are empty and I walk out onto the moor, can I be alone with the old pictures I carry in my head. Then I can spread my memories out over Hemmersmoor and find my way around. Far away from the village square and the smells that pour out of Frick's modernized kitchen, the scent of peat still hangs in the air. After dark the witches still gather on the moor. Heidrun Brodersen still struts through our streets. At night lovers meet by the canals.

Not far from the village I run into a dark figure. My first impulse is to turn off the path, but after a moment's time, I stand and wait; not too many people seek out the peat bog during a downpour.

Linde is wearing a long coat over her dress; her hair is wet and plastered to her head. "Christian," she says. "Still awake too?"

"What are you doing here?" I ask. "Why didn't you come to Frick's?"

"Do you have a cigarette?"

I offer her one but manage only after several tries to light it. Wind and rain extinguish the lighter again and again.

"I'll leave Hemmersmoor," she says suddenly, and nods several times.

"Yes," I say.

"Each and every day I walk our streets. Every day I see the same people, the same houses. But I never left. It's been like a curse—I couldn't leave."

I nod my head.

Linde takes a long drag and says, "I hope Alex gets his due and dies."

I nod again and light a cigarette for myself. "He looks pretty healthy to me."

She laughs. "Did he show you his blueprints and maps? Did you drink with him?"

"Of course," I say.

"You never had a soul." She says it without anger; she doesn't care about me. "You were always a ghost."

I nod once more. I say, "A spirit."

"You'll see. Alex will bite the dust before me."

"Sure," I say, but my answer isn't good enough for her and she turns away and leaves. She's a good friend. In her own way she's still loyal to Anke Hoffmann, as though the two were still wearing the same rolled-up braids. She's never forgiven Anke; that she owed to her friend. Her hatred bound them together, and now that Anke has died, Linde only keeps on living in her hatred for Alex. What use does she have for a new house in a new town?

What about myself? I don't have anything to forget or forgive. Nobody has ever loved me enough to hate me beyond my grave. My wife is dead, and she never knew me, couldn't see the boy from Hemmersmoor. She did away with my past like discarding a worn coat.

The chest of drawers stands in the same spot it did when I was young, and I've gathered all the old photographs. The baker Meier and my dad smile at me. They have faded, turned gray; they almost look harmless. Two young men who have just started their lives. But the dead are restless spirits—they meddle with everything. I'm a light sleeper, and they sense that and invade my dreams. This is very easy for them. I can swat at them as though they were fleas or cockroaches, but I can't get rid of them. My mother and sister keep me company and lament their fate, my housekeeping, and the state of my wardrobe. The *Gendarm* visits me, and the von Kamphoffs stop by as well. With Alex's help, their house will rise again on the hill Hüklüt the Giant left behind. All visitors gather in my living room, make themselves comfortable on the sofa and the carpet in front of the fireplace. I despise them, but if they should ever turn their backs on me, what will I have left? I was raised in this village. I can't replace them.

If I should leave Hemmersmoor once again, I won't need to burn down my house. Alex has offered to buy it, and he'll get rid of my belongings faster than any fire could. He plans to open a small boutique, maybe an antiques store. With his help, I will take all my memories with me; I will be less than a ghost. Should anybody ask about my whereabouts, Martin, Linde, and Alex will shrug helplessly and shake their heads. I can count on my old friends. Christian Bobinski, the pale boy? Never heard of him.